HEAVY

A TALE OF LOVE LOST TO THE STREETS

A NOVEL BY

Keisha Tyree

HEAVY

Book Layout: Oddball Dsgn
Cover Design: Oddball Dsgn

For further information log onto
www.ashleyjaquavis.com

Printed in the United States

Acknowledgements

OMG! This moment has been such a long time coming, excuse me while I run around my room and scream in excitement! LoL. But seriously, first and foremost, I would like to thank God for blessing me with the gift of storytelling. During the times when I seriously doubted that this profession was for me, God always found a way to remind me that it was. Writing a novel is more than just a notion, and I'm not afraid to say that many times the process left me feeling defeated. But thanks to God and the following list of people, I forged my way through until the last word was written.

To my daughter Makiya Henderson, you my love, are the brightest star to ever shine in my life. You give me the motivation and determination I need to carry on when I'm feeling low. Your smile warms my heart and your voice is like music to my ears. Although you are almost a preteen, I want you to know that you will ALWAYS be my little girl. I wish for you a lifetime of nothing but happiness and success, and I hope that I've made you proud. I love you with all that I am! Love Mommy.

To my mother, Mrs. Glenda Brown. Throughout my entire life, you have been the one person that has always remained a constant. The love and support that you show me and my sister is absolutely amazing, and I thank God for you every day. You're beautiful, kind, classy and a little bit sassy, and I want to be just like you when I grow up! Thank you for everything you do. Love you Mommy!

To my Father, Tyrell Cook, Sr. Thank you for not allowing me to grow up in this world without knowing the love of my father. Although we've had our moments, I cherish the time we spend together, and every conversation that we have. Your words of wisdom are invaluable. I admire the way you changed your life around and gave yourself over to Christ. I want you to know that I'm just as proud of you as I hope you are of me, and I love you always.

To my one and only sister, Tazana Towner. Who would have ever thought that after all those years of fighting and me trying to stab you with a butter knife (did that really happen or did I just imagine it did? LOL), that we would be as close as we are now. You are one of the few people I can depend on to drop whatever they're doing and come to my aid whenever I call. You never judge me and you always stick up for me just like an older sister should. Thank you for being another example of what an amazing woman and mother should look like. I can't wait for you to move to MD so we can turn this place out together!! #TheyAin'tReady LoL. Love you much *kisses*

To my friend and the father of my child, Ahmal Henderson. You were there on the very day when I first decided to embark on this journey. Since then, your words of encouragement have helped to carry me through. Thank you for listening to me as I bounced ideas off of you for storylines and subplots, when I know you would have much rather been watching the game. LoL. Thank you for constantly reminding me that I too could do this. Though we find ourselves apart, know that I still love you and wish for you nothing but the best. The seventeen years we spent together were some of the best times of my life and I thank you for that as well. I can't wait to see you on the big screen, papi! Love you always, K.

To some of my other biggest supporters; my cousin Patrice Watson, aka Tressie. You were the first person to ever lay eyes on this story and your feedback was definitely instrumental in helping me complete this novel. Thank you so much! To my Aunt Phyllis Berry, thank you for all your support and kind words. You've been excited about this book since the day I told you I was writing it. Thanks for helping to spread the word! To my Aunt Barbara Kelly, thank you for your support and encouragement! It means a lot to me. To my entire family; thank you!! I love every single one of y'all!

To my sisters from another mother, and my partners in crime since the 9th grade; Daphine Buggs, Takiyah Hill, Leniece Proby, Kimberly Fielder, Charla McMahan, and Neisa Townsend, I love you bishes 'til the death of me!! We've had some pretty wild times ladies. Thank you for always being down to make a few bad decisions with me. LoL. We may not talk every day, but I love each and every one of you. I'm reppin' our G-Stat clique all the way to the top! The first time I make The New York Time Bestseller List, vacay to a tropical island on ME!! Love you bishes!

I would like to say thank you to my publishers, Ashley and JaQuavis Coleman. I thought it was just a coincidence when I met one half of my favorite writing duo inside the bookstore that day. But I soon realized our meeting had to be fate. I admire the drive and work ethic in both of you. Coming from the city we're from, talent is everywhere, but very few of us ever have the opportunity to explore it. I would like to thank you both for giving me that opportunity. I am humbled to be a part of this movement and I thank both of you for allowing me to be a part. Love you much!

Shout to my label mates; Danielle Santiago, Amaleka McCall, CN Phillips, and Dream Collins. Let's take this thang all the way to the top ladies!! #TeamOWL all day!! And also a HUGE THANKS to my editor Ashley "Khloe Cain" Mustafaa. You're the bomb.com Boo and I appreciate you!

And last but certainly not least, to my future readers, THANK YOU all in advance for giving my work the time of day. I hope you enjoy reading this story as much as I did writing it. I can't wait to hear your feedback! Stay tuned for Heavy Pt. 2, coming Fall of 2013.

If you would like to keep up with events, releases and booking signings, like my Author's Page, @NovelistKeishaTyree on Facebook, or follow me on Instagram at @Keisha_Tyree. You can also keep up with the entire O.W.L team on our Facebook page @O.W.L or at www.AshleyJaquavis.com/owlhome.html.

Always love,

Keisha Tyree

Prologue

"Man, where the fuck is this nigga?" Omar questioned his cousin Jayson as the two sat inside of Omar's brand new Dodge Charger rolling a blunt. The two men had been stationed in the parking lot of the 7-Eleven on North Las Vegas Boulevard for almost twenty minutes. Big Hank, the nigga they were supposed to be meeting was still nowhere to be found.

"C'mon O, you know niggas ain't never on time. Just chill out and hit this blunt. That nigga should be here any minute." Jay said reassuringly as he handed the blunt to Omar. Jay was nervous as hell but he was trying his best not to show it. He had vouched for Hank and convinced Omar to go along with this deal even though neither of them knew much about him. This was the first time Omar had entrusted him to bring in new clientele and if anything went wrong. Jay knew his ass, and possibly even his life could end up on the line. Even though they were family, Jay was fully aware that Omar wouldn't hesitate to demote him back down to a corner boy or worse if this meeting proved to be unsuccessful.

"You know, this is exactly why I don't like fucking wit outsiders," Omar said as he put the blunt to his lips, "Niggas don't respect my muthafuckin' time. I'll give dude five more minutes then we rollin' out. I got better shit to do then to sit here waiting on some lame ass nigga." Omar stated as a thick cloud of smoke floated from his lips.

The two men continued smoking in silence as Jay nervously eyed the clock. Four minutes had passed and he

was beginning to think that Big Hank was actually going to
stand them up. But just as Omar put out the blunt and started
up the car, Jay spotted Big Hank's truck speeding into the
parking lot.

"Hold up! That's that nigga right there," Jay said pointing to the red Chevrolet Suburban that was pulling into the
convenient store's parking lot. Breathing a quick sigh of relief, Jay grabbed the oversized Louie duffel bag from the
back seat of the Charger and opened it up. Inside were twenty-five tightly wrapped bricks of pure; unstepped on Colombian cocaine, as well as, two chrome desert eagles. Jay
reached inside and took out the two throwaway pistols, handing one of them over to Omar. He put the other one down in
the waistband of his Sean John jeans and opened the car
door.

"Lemme go holla at this nigga and make sure everything is straight. I'll be right back," Jay said as he climbed
out of the car.

He wanted to make sure Big Hank wasn't on some
bullshit before he actually introduced him to Omar. After
waiting for him for more than twenty minutes, the last thing
Jay needed was for him to be short on the gwap and fuck up
the entire transaction. Omar had a lot riding on this deal. In
the five years that he'd been in Las Vegas, Omar was able to
build a stellar reputation causing his name to soon grow legs
and begin ringing bells in the streets. Because of this, about a
week ago, Omar got the call he'd been waiting on since the
day he started hustling. Sebastian Santee', a notorious Colombian drug lord who currently resided in L.A, had requested to meet with him to discuss a potential partnership. Omar
readily accepted and two days later, Santee' flew him out to
his home country of Colombia where the two of them struck
up a lucrative deal.

By eliminating the middleman and establishing a direct
connection to the product, Omar was now in a position to
cop more bricks, and he'd be doing so at much cheaper price.

If successful, the partnership was going to quickly elevate Omar to kingpin status, and Jay would be right by his side.

"Nigga, you don't know how to tell time or some shit? Why the fuck you so late?" Jay grilled Hank as soon as he climbed into the front seat of the truck.

"My bad bro, I had to handle some shit wit my triflin' ass baby moms. Bitch was on some bullshit and locked me out the house so I couldn't get my dough out the safe. I had to kick down the door at my own muthafuckin' crib. Then the crazy bitch had a nerve to pull a fuckin' gun on me," Hank said shaking his head.

Jay looked over at him like he was fuckin' nuts. *If this fat muthafucka can't even control his own bitch, how the hell he think he gonna be running the streets?* Jay thought shaking his head in amazement.

"Yeah, well, no offense my nigga, but that shit sounds like a personal problem. Make sure it doesn't happen again 'cause fam don't appreciate having to wait around on niggas when it comes to business. You feel me?"

"Fo'sho," Big Hank responded knowing he'd fucked up.

"Now, speaking of business, you got that?"

Hank nodded his head and reached underneath his seat, retrieving a large black briefcase. When he popped it open, nothing but Franklin faces stared back at the two men.

"It's all here. You wanna count it?"

"Naw, not yet," Jay said eying the briefcase. "This store is too fuckin' hot to be conducting any type of business. Follow us over to the spot."

Big Hank nodded his head and Jay hopped out of the truck and headed back over to Omar's car.

"Is everything straight?" Omar asked as he got back inside the car.

"Yeah, everything's cool. I told him to follow us over to the spot on H and McWilliams though. Shit up here is too hot."

"Good call," Omar said as he started up the car and pulled out of the parking lot. It was well after midnight but the city of Las Vegas was just starting to come alive and the traffic was extra thick. Gawking tourist and irritated residents shared the road as everybody and they mama seemed to be out looking for something to get into.

As they cruised through downtown Las Vegas, Omar puffed on the blunt and bobbed his head to Rick Ross's Teflon Don album. He wasn't really feeling the nigga Hank, but Omar was in a bind and he knew that was the only buyer Jay could find to take the bricks off his hands in such short notice. He only had forty eight hours to get rid the last of his inventory and pay off his former connect before he picked up his first shipment from Santee'. With the quality of dope Santee' was producing along with his rock bottom prices, Omar was about to make a major come up in the game.

He thought about his wife, Alaska, and how the two of them were going to be the city's most hated couple once he took his rightful place on the throne. Although he was far from a broke nigga, Omar knew teaming up with Santee' was exactly what he needed to take his operation and his paper to the next level. After diligently putting in work on the streets for the past few years, Omar now had a clientele base that stretched all the way from Las Vegas to Detroit, and everywhere in between. If he played his cards right, it wouldn't be long before he obliterated his competition and became King.

"I'm about to cause a muthafuckin' blizzard 'round dis bitch," Omar chuckled to himself as he bobbed his head and rapped along with the music. "I think I'm Big Meech/ Larry Hover/ Flippin' work/ Hallelujah..."

They finally arrived at their destination and Omar guided the Charger into the driveway of his west side stash house, shutting off the engine. He waited for Big Hank's truck to pull in behind them before he opened his door and got out. *Showtime* Omar thought as he tucked the desert eagle discreetly at his side and walked to the front door. Jay and Big Hank trailed slowly behind him. Once they got inside, Omar wasted no time getting down to business.

"Let me see dat cash," he demanded as they all stood inside the semi empty living room.

"Damn my nigga, you ain't gone even say what's up first?" Hank questioned feeling somewhat offended by Omar's cold demeanor.

"Nigga, I didn't come here to shoot the muthafuckin' shit. I came here to handle business," Omar said dismissing Hank's feelings. "So let me ask you again. What's up wit them racks my nigga?"

Jay got nervous as the two men stood there staring each other down. He placed his hand on his gun just in case Big Hank got stupid and he was forced to rectify the situation. However, he was relieved when Big Hank finally raised his hands in surrender.

"It's all good my dude. I was just trying to be courteous and shit, "Big Hank replied wearing a smirk. He then put the briefcase on top of a small round table and popped it open.

"Like I told yo mans, it's all there but you can count it if you need to."

"Fuck you mean if I need to nigga? I don't need yo muthafuckin' permission." Omar barked, testing Hank's gangsta. He hated doing business with weak ass niggas 'cause they were usually the first ones at the police station whenever some shit went down. If a nigga proved he was able to hold his own, Omar would continue to do business with him. He knew it would be less likely to come back and bite him later on.

"My bad dude, I didn't mean no disrespect." Hank said instantly bitching up.

"That's what the fuck I thought." Omar said as he plugged the first stack of hundred dollar bills into a money counting machine. His instincts told him that Big Hank was a hoe ass nigga before they had even met, but now Omar had confirmation.

I can't believe Jay brought this punk ass muthafucka to me, Omar thought to himself. He made a mental note to holla at him about the situation on the way home.

After ten minutes, the machine had counted and verified every single bill inside the briefcase, totaling four hundred thousand dollars.

"Give him the dope," Omar nodded to his cousin.

Jay quickly removed the bricks from the duffel bag and sat them on the table. He then started to replace them with the bundles of cash. While he waited, Big Hank split open one of the tightly wrapped bricks and dipped his pinky finger into the fine white powder, rubbing it across his gums.

"That's what fuck I'm talking about," Hank said as the potent drug began to numb his gums. He pulled a bag from the bottom of the now empty briefcase and began filling it up with bricks. Once the men finished loading up their respective bags, the three of them shook hands and headed to the front door. Big Hank was walking behind Omar, and Jay was at the rear. Suddenly, Omar got an overwhelming feeling that something wasn't right as he went to open the door. He instinctively reached for the desert eagle Jay gave him just as two huge goons came busting through the door. Before he even realized what was happening, Omar found himself surrounded while staring down the barrel of two .40 caliber pistols.

"Oh, my fault, I forgot to tell you," Big Hank said wearing a huge smile, "You just got GOT my nigga!"

As soon as the words left Hank's mouth, Omar realized they'd fallen for the "okey doke." He tried reaching for his gun again but it was too late. Before he could even grip the pistol's handle, Hank's goons started blazing. Multiple bullets pierced through Omar's body like a hot knife slicing through butter, and he kicked himself for not listening to his instincts. Him and Jay were completely caught off guard by the ambush and there was nothing either of them could do. As excruciating pain shot through his body, all Omar could think about was Alaska. Her beautiful caramel colored face was the last thing he saw as he collapsed to the floor in a pool of bright red blood. Jay had been hit multiple times as well, and his lifeless body was lying a few feet away from Omar's.

Hank displayed a look of complete satisfaction as he stood and surveyed the gruesome scene before him. When he snatched the duffel bag containing the money from Jay's still tightly clutched hand, Hank felt like David after he beat Goliath with his sling. Omar was about to be the man in Las Vegas and he had been the one to take him down. Hank smiled and tossed the duffel bag over his shoulder. Just as quickly as they came, the three men ran back to Hank's truck and promptly fled the scene.

CHAPTER 1

A few weeks earlier

Omar Drake stood at the one way glass window that surrounded his office and overlooked the club below. It was only eleven o'clock on the first official Friday of the summer, and Club Luxe was already doing numbers. The two thousand square feet night club was so packed, the bar was damn near out of liquor, and Omar had to place an emergency order with his distributor. As he sipped on his glass of Louis XIII, he surveyed the crowd while he waited on his team to arrive for their weekly meeting. Omar had some exciting news and he couldn't wait to share it with them. The profits from his growing drug operation, as well as, those from Club Luxe, allowed each of the men to live comfortably, but Omar's next move was about to turn that shit up.

He spotted his cousin Jay, and his best friend Mo B, as they made their way across the crowded club floor headed to his office. Omar walked over to the cherry wood desk in the center of the room and took a seat in the plush leather chair behind it. He watched the monitor and when the men arrived outside his door, he hit the button underneath his desk and buzzed them in.

"What's good fam?" Jay greeted him as soon as he walked through the door. Omar stood up and the two of them slapped hands before pulling each other in for a quick brotherly embrace.

"Shit, I can't call it," he said before turning around and sharing the same greeting with Mo B. "You niggas the ones pushing up on all that scattered ass downstairs; you tell me."

"Man!" Mo B said laughing and shaking his head. "Them hoes is out in full force tonight O, man! I don't see how you do it. There's just too many flavors of pussy out there for a nigga like me to settle down."

Jay shook his head, "You betta slow down and leave some of them hoes alone Mo. All pussy ain't good pussy my nigga."

"Shidddd," Mo B replied, begging to differ. The men laughed at his reply as they took their seats around the table. Omar was a man of few friends and his inner circle only consisted of the two men sitting in front of him. Although he had a team of goons that were explicitly loyal to him and always ready to pop off at his command, the three of them together were capable of taking down any army. Next to his wife Alaska, Jay and Mo B were the closest people to him and he trusted them with his life.

"Anyway," Omar said directing the conversation to business, "How's everything going with the eastside spots Jay? Did those niggas have any more shortages this week?"

"Naw, everything was on point. Those lil niggas actually flipped their last drop faster than I expected. I serviced Lil' Ray Ray this morning with the re-up."

"Cool," Omar nodded, turning his attention to Mo B. "What about you? Everything good on the west?"

"No doubt boss. Everything has been running smoothly."

"Excellent. I'm glad to hear everything is going well," Omar replied. He stood up and walked over to the bar; retrieving the bottle of Louis XIII he had been drinking from earlier with two more glasses. He returned to the desk and poured each of them a healthy double shot of the expensive cognac.

"Now I have a little announcement to make," Omar said handing each of them a glass.

"Well, it can't be too little if you're pulling out the good shit," Jay said putting the glass underneath his nose and sniffing it like it was wine. He inhaled the nutty, fig like aroma of the cognac before taking a small sip.

"You're right," Omar said raising his glass slightly in the air. "Today we advance to the big leagues gentlemen. I received a call today from none other than Mr. Sebastian Santee', and he has requested to meet with me about possibly starting a partnership. Now I know I don't have to tell you niggas, but if that happens, it would take this entire operation to a whole new level. His prices are rock bottom and we would have access to practically an unlimited supply of some of the best fucking dope in the country. Niggas will never be able to keep up. Before they even realize what happened, we'll be running this entire city."

"Cheers to that," Mo B said raising his glass. "Let's take this bitch over bro! Congratulations." The men each took a sip as they toasted to the possibilities.

"But this also means we have to keep our shit in order. We can't risk becoming hot while Santee' has an eye on our camp and is trying to make his decision. If we show signs of being anything other than a successful, tight knit organization, he'll walk away from the table without even so much as a second thought."

The men agreed to do everything they could to ensure their teams stayed tight during Santee's selection process. After they finished their drinks, Jay and Mo B headed back downstairs to the party, and Omar locked his office and proceeded to make his way home to his wife. It was almost two o'clock in the morning and he knew she would be asleep, but still he couldn't wait to get there so that he could climb into the bed and slide his body next to hers. Alaska had been his rock since they were both just sixteen. The product of a hustling father and a drug addicted mother, Omar's childhood was turbulent to say the least. With his mother's inability to shake the monkey off her back, and his father's back and forth stints between the penitentiary and the streets, Omar was often left alone to raise and fend for himself.

After a few run ins with the law for petty crimes like shoplifting and stealing cars, Omar seemed to be on a path to becoming a carbon copy of his father. But then he met Alaska. She was the most beautiful female specimen to ever cross his path, and at the tender age of sixteen, Omar fell in love with her. Everything about her, from her personality to the uniqueness of her name was like a breath of fresh air to him.

She grew up in a two parent home in the suburban area of their hometown of Flint, Michigan. She was the total opposite of every girl he had ever met around his way. She was funny, intelligent, and hella classy; Omar knew he had to have her. Thinking that he would have to curb his bad boy lifestyle in order to win her affection, Omar cleaned up his act and tried his best to walk the straight and narrow.

After two weeks of courting her, Alaska finally agreed to let him take her out. However, she told him that she would only do so under the condition that he quit pretending to be a choir boy because she knew that wasn't the truth. She wasn't advocating that he go out and commit any crimes, but she made it clear that she would prefer a bad boy over a sucka any day of the week. With the girl of his dreams by his side, Omar decided to try his hand at the dope game. He started out running packs for a local hustler by the name of Willie D, but he was soon promoted to a "manager" and became responsible for running Willie's entire north-side operations.

Everything was going smoothly until Omar caught a six month bid for selling dope to an undercover cop. The charge exposed his true occupation to Alaska's parents, and they promptly forbade her from ever seeing him again. She wasn't allowed to attend his trial or be there for him at his sentencing. Omar was sure that he'd lost her forever. But to his surprise, when he walked out of the Genesee County Jail five months and twenty nine days later, Alaska was right there waiting for him. She had packed a bag and gave up the secure, worry free life she enjoyed with her parents in exchange for a more exciting and adventurous one with Omar. She took direction very well, and it wasn't long before Omar made her his right hand woman. Under his guidance, she began assisting him with the cooking, cutting, and bagging process.

Once his stash reached twenty thousand racks, Omar asked Alaska for her hand in marriage. She happily accepted and the two of them packed what little belongings they had, purchased two plane tickets from Flint, Michigan to Las Vegas, never ever looking back. Omar rented a small studio apartment near the strip, and Alaska enrolled in business school while he hit the ground running, putting in major work on the streets of Las Vegas. Now, five years later, Alaska had a bachelor's degree in business from the University of Nevada Las Vegas, and Omar was officially on his way to becoming king.

As he drove through the city's still bustling streets, tomorrow's meeting with Santee' weighed heavy on his mind. He had been preparing for this moment since the day he started hustling, but he was still nervous that something could go wrong. Arriving at the entrance of his gated community, Omar entered his code on the keypad to activate the gate. He drove down the winding road until he reached their beautiful one story, Spanish-style hacienda, and he pulled into the driveway. He got out of the car and walked into the comfort of his home. As he made his way to the shower, he said a quick prayer asking the Lord to look out for him and to allow his meeting with Santee' to go smoothly. He undressed, turned the shower on full blast and allowed the steaming hot water to wash away his worries as he declared to himself that he was ready for anything.

CHAPTER 2

Alaska

Alaska woke up to find Omar's arm tightly wrapped around her body as he laid next to her in their California king sized bed snoring lightly. By the time she went to bed last night around 1:30 a.m., he still hadn't made it home yet. But she was happy to see that he was there now. In his line of business, Alaska knew that coming in late was just another part of the game. As far as she was concerned, she would rather he chase the sunrise, than to not come home at all. Alaska gently removed Omar's muscular arm from around her waist as she glanced at the clock. It was a quarter after eight and she needed to get up now if she wanted to make it to her 9:30 hair appointment in time.

She sat up on the side of the bed and slid her bare feet into her favorite pair of Gucci slippers. As she stepped down from the bed's raised platform, she yawned and raised her arms in the air, stretching her body. She made her way across the master bedroom and into the walk-in closet she shared with Omar. Larger than the average person's entire bedroom, the closet was six hundred square feet in size and comprised of completely custom shelving and shoe racks. Alaska's favorite feature however, was the island that sat in the center of the room. It had her and Omar's initials engraved on each side and it was beautifully crafted from imported cedar wood, covered in a dark cherry wood finish to match the rest of the cabinetry. It made her feel rich every time she stepped into the room.

Alaska grabbed her favorite pair of Robin jeans from the shelf along with a white rhinestone embellished tank top to match. She quickly fished out a new set of underwear and grabbed two bath towels as she made her way to the master bathroom. She quickly showered, dressed and did her makeup before emerging from the bathroom fifteen minutes later.

"Mornin' gorgeous," Omar said greeting her with a smile. He was fully awake now, sitting on the edge of the bed with his shirt off.

"Good morning baby," Alaska replied as she walked over and kissed his lips. She ran her hands across his toned chest and it made her want to climb right back in the bed and stay there with him all day.

"Where you headed?" Omar asked, wrapping his arms around her waist.

"I have a hair appointment at 9:30, then after that, Andraya and I going to do a little shopping."

"Cool," Omar said as he lovingly used his fingertips to sweep away the stray hairs that had fallen into her eye. "Do I have time to eat some breakfast before you go?"

Alaska smiled seductively. She quickly realized the kind of breakfast Omar was speaking of had nothing to do with bacon, eggs or toast. The clock on the nightstand read 9:15, but once Omar began leaving a trail of wet kisses down her stomach, Alaska became oblivious to the time. In the ten years they had been together, she had never once denied him the pleasure of making love to her and today was no different. Even when she was upset with him, she still welcomed that physical connection because it helped to remind her of what truly mattered.

"I suppose I have a little bit of time," Alaska whispered as he laid her down on the bed.

After a quick, but very efficient love making session, Alaska put her clothes back on and Omar walked her to the door.

"Good luck with your big meeting today babe. I'll see you later on tonight when you get home."

"Alright," Omar replied kissing her on the cheek. "See you then."

Alaska walked out of the salon a few hours later looking like a bag of money. Her stylist and good friend Jackie was one of the most sought after hairdressers in Las Vegas. She was the shit and she never let Alaska down when it came to hooking up her hair. Alaska was convinced that Jackie's hands had been anointed by God, and her ridiculously impeccable skills were the reason why Alaska didn't think twice when agreeing to invest fifty thousand into her new salon. While most people assumed that Alaska was just another hustler's wife, she was actually a businesswoman in her own right. As sole owner of a successful online clothing boutique, and part owner of Jackie's salon, Alaska earned enough income to support herself even though she didn't have to.

Alaska's independent spirit had been asserted early. Born to a hard-working mother of three girls, she always stressed to them the importance of having their own. She told them that doing so would ensure they never had to struggle or depend on a man to give them anything. It was a lesson that stuck and turned Alaska into the "goal" digger that she was today. Never one to be content with sitting back and not doing nothing, she always seemed to have a project or two up her sleeve.

As she climbed back inside of her Range Rover, Alaska sent her girl Andraya a text letting her know she was on her way. The two of them had become as close as two peas in a pod ever since Jay introduced them years ago. She was a breath of fresh air compared to the mindless bimbos he usually brought around and Alaska clicked with her instantly.

Both of them were originally from the east coast and seemed to have a lot in common. Alaska was born and raised in the city that boasted the country's number one murder rate; Flint, Michigan. While Andraya haled from Philly's north side.

Alaska finally arrived at the condo Andraya shared with Jay, and she pulled her truck into the spot right next to Andraya's brand new convertible Mustang GT. Before she climbed out of the car, she checked her hair and makeup in the rearview mirror out of habit. The temperature outside was ninety nine degrees in the shade, so Alaska hurriedly walked across the courtyard and rang Draya's doorbell like she was the police.

"Hurry up girl! It's hot as shit out here," she yelled through the heavy wooden door.

She was about to ring the bell again when she heard the sound of glass breaking from inside, followed by Andraya's screaming voice. Her words were inaudible and Alaska had no idea what was going on as she grabbed the spare key from under the mat and let herself in. Slowly she opened the door and was shocked to see the entire place in complete disarray. The cushions from the couches were overturned and thrown all about the room, while pieces of glass from broken picture frames littered the floor. Alaska glanced toward the balcony and she could see pieces of Jay's wardrobe hanging over the edge. *"Wow,"* she whispered as she stepped inside and shut the door behind her. "He must have really fucked up this time."

As she walked deeper inside the condo, Alaska tried to call out to her friends and let them know she was there, but their heated argument left them totally unaware of her presence.

"You. Fuckin'. Disgust. Me." Andraya said spewing her words slowly and clearly, while lacing them with every ounce of hate her soul could muster. "I spend the better part of my days cooking, cleaning and catering to yo bum ass, and now you're telling me that not only have you been fucking this ratchet ass broad, but now you done got the hoe pregnant? Like, you actually ran up in her dusty ass raw, then came back home to me? Your trifling ass didn't even respect me enough to strap up, you dirty dick muthafucka." Andraya was beyond pissed. The hurt and disappointment she felt radiated through in her voice.

"But bay," Jay replied, finally able to get a word in. He spoke in the softest voice Alaska had ever heard on a man, but still Andraya shut him down.

"Don't fucking bay me, nigga. Just get your shit and get the hell out. RIGHT FUCKING NOW!"

Alaska expected for Jay to protest against her demands once more, but his words never came. Instead he rounded the corner and came into the living room with his shoulder sunken and his expression somber. He was so caught up in what had just went down that he didn't even notice Alaska until he was standing directly in front of her.

"'Laska!" Jay said, shocked to see her standing there. "Uhh …What are you doing here, ma?"

Alaska could see the embarrassment written on his face as he realized she'd just overheard everything that went down between him and Draya.

"I… uhh… I came to pick up Draya for the spa and shopping day we had planned," Alaska answered, feeling slightly uncomfortable.

Jay was like family to her and Draya was her best friend. She didn't want to take sides, but if she had to, she was rolling with her girl all day on this one. Cheating was one of her biggest pet peeves, especially when the woman being cheated on has been nothing short of a ride or die chick for her man. It just didn't make any sense to her, and no matter who tried to explain it, she just couldn't wrap her brain around the concept of knowingly hurting the one you claim to love. As he stood there with his eyes cast to the floor and unable to look her in the eyes, Alaska had to fight the urge to tell him how trifling and out cold he had been for his actions.

She knew it wasn't exactly her place, but even more so than that, she held her tongue because she could already see the regret in Jay's eyes so she just left it alone. The two of them stood there for what felt like forever, until Jay finally broke the silence.

"I'm so sorry, sis," he said, kissing the side of her cheek. "I'm going to grab a room at the Wynn for the rest of the night. Take care of her for me, okay?"

Alaska only nodded as she watched Jay walk out the door. Taking a deep breath, she walked over to the mini bar and grabbed an unopened bottle of wine from the cooler. She then located the cork remover and grabbed two wine glasses before heading to the condo's master bedroom to comfort her girl.

CHAPTER 3

Andraya sat on the side of the bed with her head in her hands. She was so jaded to Jay's constant infidelities that she couldn't even cry anymore. The anger and hurt she felt weighed heavy on her heart, but her mind wouldn't allow the tears to fall. In all the years that they'd been together, Jay stepped out on Draya more times than she could count, and each time she forgave him and took him back. But this time was different. Having a baby outside of their marriage was the ultimate sign of disrespect and she refused to stand for it. Especially, when the bitch he knocked up couldn't even hold a torch to Draya on her best fucking day.

Draya was trying to get her breathing to return back to normal when she heard sounds coming from the kitchen. She could have sworn she heard the front door close, but her anger returned instantly as she realized Jay must've still been inside the house. "This nigga must think I'm a fuckin joke," Andraya said as she jumped up from the bed and practically sprinted towards the kitchen.

"I thought I told you to get the fuck out!" Andraya screamed as she came around the corner nearly colliding with Alaska.

"Oh my God, Alaska?" Andraya said, shocked to see her best friend. "Girl, what are you doing here?"

"I was coming to pick you up for our spa day, remember?"

"Oh yeah," Andraya said as she embarrassingly looked around the war-torn room, "I'm sorry, I forgot all about that 'Laska."

"Don't worry, it's cool."

Andraya noticed the wine bottle and two glasses dangling from Alaska's hands. "Have you been here long?" she asked, wondering how much of she and Jay's conversation Alaska had heard.

"No, I just got here," Alaska lied. Being cheated on was humiliating enough without having to feel like everybody knew your business. She knew Draya was going to give her the blow by blow of happened anyway, so she figured she might as well let her do so. "I rang the bell, but when you didn't answer I just used the spare key. Then I walked in and seen this mess, so I figured a bottle of wine was going to be in order."

Andraya looked at her friend and smiled, "Thank you girl. I don't know how you do it, but you're always there when I need you the most. However," Draya said grabbing the bottle of wine from Alaska's hand, "I'm going to need something a little bit stronger than wine."

The girls shared a laugh as Andraya walked over to the wet bar and switched the wine bottle with a fifth of Patrón. "Now that's more like it," she said as she grabbed two shot glasses and walked back over to Alaska. The living room area was a mess so she decided it would be better if they held court in her bedroom. Andraya led the way and Alaska followed close behind. Once they were inside, Alaska made herself right at home removing her shoes and plopping down on the king size bed in the center of the room. Andraya pored each of them a double shot before sitting down on the bed to join her.

"I'm moving back to Philly," she announced as she tilted her head back swallowing the contents of the glass in one gulp before immediately pouring herself another one.

8

"What?! Why?" Alaska asked with a full shot glass still in her hand. "You can't just leave me here in this city all by myself. Philly is like a million miles away!"

"I know 'Laska, I'm sorry. And believe me, I really don't want to. But I can't stay here and continue playing the fool for this man. I have to draw the line somewhere, you know?"

Alaska sighed before finally consuming her shot. "Yeah, I feel you girl. But are you sure y'all can't work things out? I mean, no shade, but what's so different about this time?"

"Jay got Vanessa pregnant," Andraya confessed downing her third shot. There was no need for her to explain who Vanessa was, for as long as Draya had been around, Vanessa had been there too. She was a constant thorn in the side of their relationship, and just like an incurable herpes virus, she never seemed to go away. "Can you believe that nigga was dumb enough to fuck her raw? I mean, the bitch is only nineteen for Christ fucking sake! Meanwhile, my dumb ass is running around this bitch playing Suzie Homemaker." Andraya shook her head at the twisted irony.

"Damn, girl. I don't even know what to say," Alaska replied, pouring herself another shot. "I don't think you should go back to Philly if that's not truly where you want to be though. Stay here and remind that nigga everyday what he'll be missing. If you want, you can even stay with me and Omar until you find yourself a place."

"Thank you so much, Alaska." Draya reached across the bed and gave her a hug. "I truly appreciate that."

The room became silent as Draya took another shot and became lost in her thoughts. She glanced out the window at the plush flower covered courtyard and wondered if she really should stay. Her life in Philly had been a hard one and once she left, she swore she would never go back. But she knew living in Vegas without a job and no man to support her, wouldn't exactly be a walk in the park either. Still, the thought of going back home in the same position she was in when she left overwhelmed her.

Andraya never had a friend like Alaska and she truly valued their friendship. As the two of them continued to down their shots, Draya weighed the pros and cons of staying there with Jay. She loved him to death but there was only so much her heart could take. She was simply fed up. Deciding that she needed some space, Draya got up and went to the closet to grab her suitcase.

"You know what," Draya said as she began throwing clothes inside the Louis Vuitton luggage. "I think I'll take you up on that offer,"

Alaska smiled as she stood up and began to help her friend pack. She was proud of her girl for standing her ground, but she couldn't help but wonder how long it would last. Jay was a smooth talker and every time Draya tried to leave him, he always found a way to talk her off the ledge.

After Draya filled up her luggage with everything she thought she might need, she wrote a letter to Jay explaining that she needed some time to think. She told him she would be staying at Alaska's, and that she would contact him when and if she was ready to talk. Leaving the letter on the nightstand, Andraya took one more shot before she grabbed her suitcase and walked out of the door.

CHAPTER FOUR

Omar was unusually nervous as he drove his Escalade slowly down the tarmac of a private airstrip located thirty miles outside of Las Vegas. He received a call at 6:30 this morning informing him that Santee' needed to take an unexpected trip back to his homeland, and if Omar was still interested in meeting with him, he would have to fly to Medellin, Colombia in order to do it. The good news was that Santee' would charter a private jet for him to get there, but the bad news was that Omar was scared to fly. As he drove further down the tarmac, Omar could see the G5 Gulf Stream jet sitting on the runway. The jet's expansive wingspan made Omar even more nervous as he pulled up next to it and parked his truck. He hadn't flown since he was just a little boy, and that experience had turned out to be a traumatic one.

Omar said a prayer and took a deep breath as he climbed out of the car. As soon as he stepped foot on the pavement, a gentleman dressed in a black suit with white gloves appeared at his side.

"Good morning Mr. Drake. May I take your bags, sir?"

"Uh… yeah sure," Omar said, handing the man his Louis Vuitton duffle bag. He'd never flown private before but already he could tell it was the shit. Santee' was balling on a level very few hustlers ever got to experience. His lifestyle was ten times more lavish than that of your favorite rapper or athlete, and his name commanded more respect in the streets than The President of the United States. Simply put, Santee' was "The Man" and Omar couldn't wait to get on his level.

A red strip of carpet led the pathway to the jet's stairs, and Omar walked along it amazed at how much Santee's had gone all out. He ascended the small staircase, counting each one of the fifteen steps as he went along, trying to calm his nerves. Once he reached the top of the staircase and stepped onto the plane, he was greeted by another member of the flight staff. This time it was a beautiful Spanish woman with long dark hair and banging curves. Omar's nerves instantly went away when she reached out to shake his hand.

"Welcome aboard Mr. Drake. My name is Gabriella and I'll be your personal stewardess today. Please take your seat and make yourself comfortable. The pilot is completing the plane's pre-flight check, but once he's finished we'll be taking off to our final destination of Medellin, Colombia. Please let me know if you need anything in the meantime, okay?" Omar smiled at the sexy Colombian stewardess and nodded his head. Her Spanish accent was thick and he struggled to understand everything she said, but he was still able to get the gist of it.

"Is it possible for me to get a drink while we're waiting for takeoff?" Omar asked needing something strong to help mellow him out for the long eight hour flight.

"Of course sir, we have a fully stocked bar on board. What can I get you?"

"You got any Bacardi 151?" He asked, and Gabriella nodded her head in approval. "Let me get a straight shot, no chaser. Matter fact, just gimme a double," Omar decided.

He knew the powerful liquor would be just what he needed to relax his mind and help him get through this trip. As Gabriella went over to the bar to prepare his drink, Omar began looking around the massive jet and was truly impressed with what he saw. The jet's lavish décor, state-of-the-art technology, and top of the line equipment, was a blatant sign of Santee's wealth and power and Omar hoped to one day reach his future boss level.

Gabriella bought over his drink and Omar only got half of it down before he felt the effects of the extremely potent liquor start to take over his body. The tension in his neck and shoulders finally began to subside and his muscles relaxed as he leaned his head back on the headrest and closed his eyes. His thoughts immediately drifted back to Alaska as he wondered what his wife was doing. The spur of the moment trip meant that he had to cancel their plans for a weekend getaway to Lake Tahoe, and Omar hoped she wasn't too vexed about it. Though Alaska always understood when things came up, she wasn't always as forgiving to the fact.

Omar pulled out his phone to give her a call, but the pilot's voice came over the speaker announcing their departure, so he decided to text her instead.

Hey Love, we're about to take off. Just wanted to say I love you and I'm sorry about the Lake Tahoe trip. I promise I'll make it up to you though. Love you always, TTYL :).

Send.

Omar heard the roar of the jet's engines as they came to life at the push of a button. Slowly the massive machine maneuvered around the tarmac until it was aligned perfectly with the runway. With no other traffic at the private airstrip, the jet took off and began its gradual ascend to fifty thousand feet almost immediately. The shot of Bacardi 151 running through his veins along with the pressure of gravity weighing down on his body as they elevated, forced Omar's eyes to shut as he leaned his head further back onto the headrest. Sleep soon followed.

Several hours into the flight, Omar was still asleep as he dreamt about making love to his wife while Gabriella sat in a chair next to the bed and watched. Alaska was on all fours as she crawled across the bed and proceeded to wrap her juicy lips around his big black dick. She expertly began to deep throat all nine inches of him as she moved her mouth slowly up and down his thick, long shaft. With her right hand free, Alaska located his g-spot and began to lightly tickle the area between his ass and his nuts. The sensation damn near caused Omar to bust right there on the spot as pre cum oozed from the head of his dick while Alaska quickly lapped it all up. He knew he wouldn't be able to hold back his nut much longer, so Omar instructed her to get up and turn around as he prepared to enter her from behind. Right as he placed his dick to the opening of her dripping wet vagina, he was startled awake by the feeling of actual wetness on his dick.

"Whoa!" Omar opened his eyes to find Gabriella on her knees in between his legs with his dick in her hands. "Yo, ma, what the fuck are you doing?" Her lips were just inches away from his manhood and he could feel the warmth of her breath as she brushed up against it. He wanted so badly to slide his piece inside of her mouth, but Omar didn't know exactly what relation Gabriella was to Santee' so he had to be careful. The last thing he needed was to mess around and fuck the boss's daughter or some crazy shit like that. He wasn't trying to risk his chances of becoming connected by fucking up and hitting some forbidden pussy.

"It's okay papi," Gabriella purred, "Just sit back and close your eyes. Santee' paid me very well to take good care of you, and I fully intend to give you his money's worth."

Naturally, Omar's x-rated dream left him horny as hell and since his dick was already rock hard, he decided to just lay back and let Gabriella do her work. He figured he could release some tension before his big meeting, and Gabriella would be doing the job she was paid to do; it was a win-win situation for everybody. Not long after she began working her magic, Omar felt that familiar tingle in the bottom of his stomach signaling that he was about to cum. He opened his eyes in order to see Gabriella as she swallowed his babies, but he was met instead with the barrel of the pilot's chrome desert eagle pointed directly in his face.

Omar's dick instantly went limp. "What the fuck!?" he said through clenched teeth. He had no idea what was going on and that angered him even more as he eyed the two of them for answers that would never come. Without saying a single word to him, Gabriella stood to her feet, wiped her mouth and glanced over at the pilot.

"Shoot him." She demanded. Her words were casual and devoid of any emotions. Omar tried to protest, but before he could say another word, the pilot did as he was told and pulled the trigger.

POP!!

The sound of Gabriella popping the cork on a bottle of Krug Rose' jolted Omar from his nightmare as he jumped up drenched in sweat.

"Mr. Drake! I'm glad to see you're finally awake," Gabriella said smiling. "And your timing is perfect. We'll be landing in about ten minutes so I'll need you to sit back down and fasten your seat belt. One of Mr. Santee's associates will be meeting us on the tarmac, and they asked that I give you a bottle of champagne to take down to the car." Gabriella handed Omar a chilled ice bucket with the champagne bottle she just opened and two glasses tucked down inside.

"I hope you enjoyed the flight Mr. Drake. I'll see you back here tomorrow morning for our departure." Gabriella smiled as she took her seat and strapped herself in preparing for landing.

"Thanks," was all Omar managed to get out as he sat there still trying to shake off the crazy dream he'd just had.

The plane landed and as soon as the pilot let down the doors, Omar grabbed the ice bucket along with his duffle bag and quickly raced down the steps. He was glad to finally be back on solid ground, but his nerves were now worse than ever due to the fucked up dream he had on the plane. As he walked over to the chauffeur driven Maybach, Omar knew he needed to pull it to together. He didn't want to start the meeting off on the wrong foot by appearing nervous, so he forced his mind to return to its normal state of calm. Men like Santee' enjoyed preying on the weak and Omar had no plans on being his next victim.

Omar finally reached the luxury vehicle and again, out of nowhere, the man in the black suit and white gloves appeared to open the door for him.

"Thanks bro," Omar nodded as he tossed his duffle bag into the backseat of the car then slid his body down onto the plush interior. It was his first time inside of a Maybach, but he vowed it would not be his last. He ran his hand over the butter soft leather seats as he began to admire all the car's many amenities. Omar was so captivated by the car's beauty that he almost forgot to acknowledge his fellow passenger. When he looked to his left, Omar didn't expect to see one of the most beautiful women he'd ever seen in his life, but there she was. Her smooth skin was the color of caramel macchiato, and her jet black hair was pulled up into a bun at the top of her head. She wore an all-white suit with a low cut jacket, and a skirt short enough to show almost her entire thigh when she sat down. Five inch Louboutins adorned her feet, and Chanel No.5 emitted from her pores. Next to his wife, she was the second baddest woman he'd ever seen hands down.

"Omar Drake, I presume?"

He nodded and she stuck out her hand for him to shake. "Sophia Smith; It's a pleasure to meet you.

"Same here," Omar said as he held onto her insanely soft hand a few seconds longer than he needed to.

Sophia smiled at him coyly as she cleared her throat and politely pulled her hand away from his. "Santee sends his apologies for not being able to meet you upon your arrival. However, he should be ready to see you as soon as we get to the house. I trust that everything with your flight was up to par?"

"Absolutely, and I truly appreciate the hospitality."

"Excellent," she said, before redirecting her attention to her buzzing iPhone. "Excuse me for a moment."

Omar nodded and turned his focus to the scenery outside his window. Colombia was an exceptionally beautiful country and he soaked in all the breathtaking views attempting to commit them to his memory as they passed by his window. After a few minutes, she finished up with her conversation.

"Your first time here in Colombia?" she asked, snapping Omar from his daze.

"Yes, and I must say, it's absolutely beautiful here."

"Si'," she said, agreeing with his statement, "but most of the living conditions here are in stark contrast to that very same environment."

"Really? That's sad," Omar replied. "Do you live here?"

"No. I live and work alongside Santee' back in Las Vegas, but Medellin is my birthplace. I lived here until the age of five when the streets became too dangerous for my family to live."

The two of them continued to engage in small talk as they enjoyed the thirty minute drive to Santee's El Poblado compound. Right before they arrived, Omar checked his cell phone for the first time and saw that he had seven missed calls, all from his cousin Jay. He excused himself just as Sophia did earlier and called him back. Omar knew something must have been important for Jay to call him that many times in a row, and he prayed nothing was wrong with Alaska as he waited for his cousin to answer.

"Yo, O! Sorry to interrupt bro, but we got a situation. Them niggas representing the eastside blocks we took over last month, done robbed and shot up the spot over there on Myrtle. Lil' Marko is dead and there's police all over the place. Me and Mo B got a tail on them niggas though. I know you wanted to keep shit quiet until you got back, but all you have to do is say the word my nigga, and we can eliminate the problem right now."

"Go," Omar simply said before tapping the red box on his screen to end the call. He didn't even have to think twice about clapping back on them niggas. His only hope was that Jay and Mo B were able to handle the situation before Santee' was ever able to get wind of it.

Omar finally looked up from his phone and he found himself awestruck for what felt like the millionth time that day. Santee's massive compound was something out of a Hollywood movie, and Omar's eyes darted back and forth as he discreetly tried to take it all in. He estimated the entire property to be about the size of four football fields. The driveway was paved with perfectly laid cobblestone slabs, and from his seat inside the Maybach, Omar could see the main house, as well as, the three larger than average guest houses surrounding it. The landscaping immaculately showcased vivid shades of greens, reds, oranges and yellows, and a few others Omar had never seen before. Since his arrival, the only thing he'd seen that was more striking than the landscape was the lovely Ms. Sophia. He was reminded again by the fact when she touched his arm and snapped him out of his daze.

"Are you okay?" she asked, one leg out the door as the chauffeur held it open.

"Yeah, I'm cool ma. I was just admiring the scenery."

Sophia smiled, "C'mon, let's go inside." She said climbing out of the car.

Omar did the same and he trailed closely behind her as they walked up the designated pathway to the house. The massive wooden doors on the front of the house had to be at least twenty feet tall, and Omar could tell they were heavy by the way the butler used both hands to pull one of them open.

"Hola Pablo," Sophia greeted the older Colombian man with a kiss on the cheek. "This is Mr. Drake." She moved to the side so that the men could shake hands.

"Hola, Mr. Drake." Pablo spoke with a heavy Spanish accent. He motioned for Omar to raise his hands in the air and then he proceeded to pat him down in search of any weapons or wires he may have been carrying. When he was satisfied Omar was clean, he continued his welcome. "Right this way. El senor Santee is waiting for the two of you in his office."

Omar nodded and he followed Sophia and Pablo to the second floor and down a long hallway that led to Santee's office. When they arrived outside the door, Pablo knocked on it twice signaling their arrival. Omar took a deep breath and put his game face on, readying himself for the biggest meeting of his life.

"Come in." Santee's booming voice crept through the door. Pablo opened it, allowing Sophia and Omar to enter.

Just as Omar expected, the office was much more lavish than anything he'd ever seen before. Everything from the furniture to the cherry wood floors appeared to be top of the line with absolutely no expense spared.

"Omar, my friend. It is so good to finally meet you." Santee stood up from behind his executive style desk and walked over to shake Omar's hand.

"Likewise," Omar assured, "and thank you for inviting me into your home."

Santee' nodded. "Please, have a seat." He said gesturing toward the leather seats situated directly in front of his desk before taking his own. "Sophia, can you bring us a bottle of cognac from the bar please?"

Omar relaxed as he eased his body into the incredibly soft leather chair. Surprisingly, once he was in Santee's presence all his nerves dissipated and he was ready to do business. They waited for Sophia to retrieve the bottle. Once everybody had their drinks Santee' got right to business.

"So, Omar," Santee' finally spoke after taking the first sip of his drink. "I understand you would like to do business together, is that correct?"

8

"It is," Omar replied confidently. "I'm at the top of my game in these streets, and now I'm ready to take my operation to the next level. The demand of my clientele has outgrown my current supplier, and I need a distributor of your caliber in order to keep up."

"I see. And how many bricks do you typically move in a months' time?" Santee asked while lighting one of his favorite Cuban cigars.

"A hundred plus; but I guarantee you I can double that if you put me on."

"How many men do you have on your team?"

"About fifteen or so," Omar estimated.

"And how many of them do you believe are unconditionally loyal?"

"Two."

Santee' nodded as he took another puff of his cigar then continued, "Ever caught a case and beat it?"

"I caught an intent to sell charge when I was younger. I didn't beat it, but I served my time, got out, and I've successfully flown under the radar ever since."

Omar finished his spiel but Santee' just remained expressionless as he continued to enjoy his cigar. Smoke bellowed from his mouth in "O" shaped rings, and he amusingly watched them as they floated into the air. His line of questioning had been unexpected, but Omar had no problem keeping up. Anxious, he glanced over at Sophia as he waited for Santee' to say something. She caught his glance and discreetly winked her eye, ensuring him that everything was okay.

"I work on consignment," Santee' finally spoke after what seemed like forever. "When you place an order, payment has to be delivered to me in full and within two weeks. Failure to do so will make the deal null and void. The ticket is 16.5 per kilo, with a minimum purchase of fifty. Any order of a hundred or more, drops the ticket down to 15.5." Santee' took another brief pause, and Omar could have sworn he heard his rapid heartbeat echoing throughout the room in the silence. The keys to his empire had just been officially cut and handed to him on a diamond key ring. Omar was ecstatic.

"All orders must be placed forty-eight hours in advance," Santee' continued," and Sophia will give you the contact information of the man you'll need to contact to do so. Pickup and drop off points will be conducted at separate and different undisclosed locations with each transaction. Make sure you have a transport team ready and willing to travel when your orders come in. Think you can handle all that?"

"Without a doubt," Omar replied cool and confidently.

"Well then, welcome to the team." Santee raised his glass and Omar and Sophia followed suit. "To prosperity and new partnerships." The three of them tapped their glasses together.

"Salute!!" they all echoed in unison.

CHAPTER FIVE

Jay and Mo B followed the niggas who shot up the eastside spot to a house that was located in a suburban neighborhood not too far from the strip. Jay could tell when he got a glimpse at the shooters that they were just young kids, and the house they were now sitting in front of preparing to light up like a Christmas tree, very likely belonged to the kids' parents. Still, that didn't stop Jay from carrying out his order. Kids or no kids, their violations to organization would not be tolerated. Mo B took the AR-15 assault rifle from its case and loaded the clip. Jay pulled the black stocking he was wearing down over his face. Then he pulled the hammer back on his desert eagle, forcing a bullet into the gun's chamber.

He looked over at Mo B and asked, "You ready my nigga?" Mo B gave a quick nod and just like that, the men stepped out of the car and began turning the front of the house into swiss cheese. They fired their guns into the house in the same brazen manor the young boys had used on them. Once his magazine was empty, Mo B hopped back in the car waiting for Jay to finish. It was late at night and they were in a suburban area, helping to enhance the probability that the police were already on their way. Still, after he put his gun in the back seat, Mo B turned around to find Jay walking towards the house instead of the car.

"Nigga, what the fuck are you doing?" he called out. "We gotta get the fuck on down. Dem boys gone be here any minute."

"Take the car and meet me at the spot in ten minutes." Jay said over his shoulder.

"But …"

"Just do it!" Jay spat, cutting Mo B's protest off before it even began. Shooting up the house the way they did was meant to send a message. But Jay also wanted to ensure that the job was complete and in order to do that, he had to go inside. Creeping around to the back of the house, Jay checked the patio door and found that it was unlocked. He slid the glass door open a few inches listening for any movement inside. When he didn't hear anything, he opened the door wider and stepped inside.

The patio opened up to the kitchen, and as Jay walked further into the house he could smell the unmistakable metallic like scent of fresh blood in the air. With his gun drawn, he rounded the corner to the living room where he found three motionless bodies lying on the floor. Two of them belonged to their intended targets, but the last one was that of a little girl, no more than five or six years old. Naturally, the sight of her lifeless body tugged at Jay's heartstrings and he was instantly felt a twinge of regret. He bent down over the girl's body and began to recite the Lord's Prayer when he saw a slight movement out the corner of his eye.

Jay whipped around preparing to shoot anything that moved, but instead he was caught by surprise when he found himself staring down the barrel of a gun.

"You killed my babies!" screamed the petite, dark skin woman on the other side of the gun. Jay could see the rage in her eyes and he knew he had to act quickly. Even though he was strapped, the fact that her gun was trained on him and his was on the floor at his feet, left him at a bit of a disadvantage Raising his arms into the air, Jay said the first thing that popped into his head.

"It wasn't me, I swear." Jay lied. "I heard the shots from down the street and I ran down here to make sure everyone was okay."

The distraught mother paused and cocked her head to one side as she curiously looked Jay in his eyes. She appeared to be buying his story when all of a sudden; she surprised him by letting off two wild shots. One hit Jay in the right arm, and the other grazed his right leg.

"Liar!" She cried as Jay gripped his arm in pain. "I saw you out of my bedroom window. You killed my innocent babies, now I'm going to kill you too." She raised the gun and took aim directly at Jay's chest. Knowing she wasn't that good of a shooter, Jay took a chance and dived to the floor just as she pulled the trigger. He waited to hear the explosion from the gun followed by the burning sensation of a bullet piercing his flesh, but it never came. Realizing that her gun was empty, Jay quickly grabbed his from the floor and he expertly fired off a single round, striking her in the head.

As she dropped to the floor, Jay could hear the police sirens wailing in the distance. He hurriedly wrapped his arm in a Dora the Explorer blanket that he found draped over the couch, and he exited the bullet ridden house the same way he came. Running through backyards and jumping fences, Jay cleared the four blocks to the meeting spot in less than five minutes. Just as they planned, Mo B had ditched the car they used in the shooting, and he was now waiting for Jay in a black, newer model BMW.

"My nigga, what happened to you?" Mo B asked as Jay climbed into the car. The Dora blanket was soaked in blood, and his face and clothes were dripping with sweat from his run over.

"Long story," Jay replied. "I'll tell you all about it later. But for now, let's just get the fuck up out of here."

Jay sent Omar a text letting him know the job was done, and then leaned his head back onto the headrest as Mo B shifted the car into gear and peeled off.

HEAVY

Back in his hotel room, Jay's arm was now bandaged and nestled in a sling as Vanessa sat positioned on her knees in front of him with her mouth around his dick. She expertly sucked his muscle as Jay thought about the argument he and Andraya had earlier. Although he loved Draya, he just couldn't stop himself from indulging in other women. He had a weakness for them ever since he was just a teenage boy. And if he had to be painfully honest with himself, Jay didn't see that changing any time soon. He truly wanted to be with Draya, and Jay was happy that he'd married her. But he needed her to understand that she would probably never be the only woman in his life. He knew it was a hard sell, but women rolled with it all the time. Especially if the man they were with had money.

Vanessa noticed that Jay seemed distracted, so she purposely let her teeth drag along his dick.

"Watch your teeth, ma," Jay snapped out of his trance, stiff arming her forehead as he pulled his dick from inside her mouth. "You know I don't like that shit."

"Well then you need to start concentrating on this muthafuckin' blow job I'm giving you, and stop daydreaming about them other hoes."

"Watch yo' mouth," Jay said putting his dick back inside his pants. "And you don't know what the fuck I was thinking about."

"Oh really?" Vanessa smirked, standing to her feet. "Enlighten me then."

"I was actually thinking about the fact that neither one of us is ready to have a baby. I mean you're only nineteen, you haven't even finished high school yet, and I'm too busy out here in these streets to be looking after some snot nose little kid."

Vanessa looked at him in disgust as she put her hands on her hips and rolled her eyes. "We've already been through this. I'm not getting an abortion, Jay. You're the one always insisting we fuck without a condom, so you're going to deal with the consequences and figure out a way to make this shit work just like me."

"But it would be so much better if we waited," Jay said standing up and looking her in the eye. He was willing to say anything to get her to abort the baby so that he could repair things with Draya, and hopefully they could move on.

"Wait for what, Jay? The moon and the stars to perfectly align in the sky?"

"No, baby, just until you graduate from high school and turn twenty-one. That way we can do this thing the right way and have a big wedding in front of all your friends."

Jay could see the wheels spinning in her head at the mention of a wedding, and he knew he almost had her.

"You really want to marry me?" Vanessa smiled as she took a few steps closer.

"Of course I do baby. I just want us to do it the right way."

"But what about your wife? And what if I get the abortion and something goes wrong? I've heard all kind of horror stories from my girls about chicks who've had abortions and now they can never get pregnant again."

"Don't worry about that," Jay said pulling her into his arms. "I'll make sure the procedure is performed by the best doctor money can buy. You just say the word and I'll set it all up. You won't have to worry about anything." He conveniently skipped over her question about Draya, but she was so into her thoughts, she didn't even notice.

Vanessa pulled away from him and looked down at the floor. The baby she was carrying was her ace in the hole, and it was the only way she could ensure her place in Jay's life. While she wanted nothing more than to be his wife, Vanessa knew she couldn't trust him to keep his word.

"Just let me think about it, okay? I'll get back with you in a couple of days." Vanessa grabbed her purse and she kissed Jay on the cheek before heading to the door. "I'll call you later," she said over her shoulder.

Once Jay heard the door close behind her, he flopped back down on the couch releasing a deep breath.

"Bitches," he said, shaking his head.

CHAPTER SIX

After finalizing the details of their partnership, Santee', Omar and Sophia enjoyed a dinner of filet mignon and main rock lobster tails inside of Santee's formal dining room. The conversation between them was effortless and it shifted to many different topics throughout the night, giving one the impression that the three of them had been friends for years. Omar was getting a history lesson on Santee's rise in the game, and he learned that the kingpin had started out working as a runner for the infamous Pablo Escobar when he was just twelve years old. Under Escobar's reign, Santee's desire to become King was ignited. He quickly learned the ropes, putting in work in every area from packaging to murder.

By the time he turned nineteen, Escobar had been toppled by the Colombian government and Santee' had taken it upon his self to pick up the leftover pieces. Slowly but surely, Santee' built up quite an impressive organization which spanned across several Colombian cities. At the age of twenty-one, Santee' partnered with several major U.S. distributors and took his empire international.

"And the rest," Santee' said, placing his napkin on top of his now empty plate, "is history."

"Wow," Omar replied. "That's one hell of a story."

"Indeed it is," Sophia finally spoke. "And it only gets better after you've heard it a thousand and one times." She joked, rolling her eyes playfully towards the sky.

The men laughed at her joke as she stood up from the table, smoothing down her skirt.

"Well Mr. Drake, I'm sure you must be tired from the long flight you had today," Sophia said as she walked around the table. "You'll be staying in the main guesthouse this evening. I believe Pablo already has everything set up for you there."

"Awesome. Just point me in that direction," Omar replied, rising from his chair.

"It's just a short walk around the back and through the garden. But I can walk you over there if you'd like." Her smile caused Omar's energy level to perk up.

"Actually, I would like that," he replied matter-of-factly.

Grabbing his bag, Omar turned his attention to Santee'. "It was a pleasure to meet you. Thank you for welcoming me on and I can't wait to start getting this money."

"Si' my friend, same here. Sophia will contact you soon with the details of your first shipment. Until then, be well amigo."

The two men shook hands then Omar followed Sophia out of the door.

"You did well in there," Sophia complimented as they strolled through the garden.

"Thanks," Omar replied. He'd been nervous when he was first introduced to Santee', and he was glad she hadn't noticed. As they continued their stroll, Omar purposely slowed down his pace in an effort to extend their time together. Although Alaska was still in the back, front and sides of his mind, Omar couldn't deny the natural attraction he felt towards Sophia.

"I can't get over how beautiful it is here," Omar marveled. "When I retire, this is where I want to be."

"Mmm," she nodded with her lips pressed together. "Well, when you're ready let me know. I can refer you to some awesome realtors."

"Bet," Omar chuckled knowing that day would probably be several years away.

"Well, here we are."

As the two of them approached the door, Omar tried to quickly think of a reason to keep her in his presence.

"Damn," Omar said looking disappointed, "Already? I was really enjoying your company. Would you like to come in and have drink with me?" Omar asked, not even knowing if the guesthouse had been stocked with liquor or not.

"Sure, why not. I'm sure Pablo thought to leave a bottle or two somewhere in there."

Sophia bent down to retrieve the guesthouse key from under the mat. She unlocked the door then handed Omar the key as she stepped inside. "Just put it back under the mat or leave it on the counter when you leave," she instructed.

Omar nodded as he stepped inside and sat his bag down by the door. Sophia proceeded to give him a quick tour before checking the bar to see if Pablo had stocked any liquor.

"Bingo," Sophia called out when she found bottles of Ciroc, Patron, Remy VSOP and Hennessy neatly lined up in a row behind the bar. "What's your preference?" she asked, informing him of his choices.

"I'll take the Ciroc."

Sophia placed the Ciroc, a small bottle of papaya juice some ice and two glasses on a tray and walked it over to the living room area where Omar was now sitting.

"Here you are, Mr. Drake.," she smiled as she put the tray down. "Now would you like that straight or with a splash of papaya?"

"Straight. And timeout on that Mr. Drake shit. You can call me Omar, ma."

"Okay then, Omar," Sophia playfully emphasized as she handed him his drink. "Tell me more about you."

Omar proceeded to give her the condensed version of his life story, conveniently, but unconsciously leaving out the fact that he was married.

"Have you spoken with your parents at all since you left your hometown?" Sophia asked wondering what it must be like for someone to grow up and not have either parent in their life.

"Actually I have. My mother has been clean for the last year and a half and since then, we've grown closer. My father unfortunately was murdered three years ago."

"Oh, well that's good ... About your mother, not your father," Sophia said clarifying her statement. The effects of all the drinks she'd consumed within the last few hours were slowly sneaking up on her.

"I knew what you meant," Omar smiled, placing his arm behind her head on the couch. "Now it's your turn. Tell me how a beautiful and intelligent woman like you, became the right hand to a man like Santee'."

"By being just that," Sophia answered, referring to the attributes he'd just given her. "I was initially brought on as the first member of Santee's all female team, the Cocaine Housewives. From there I got to showcase my expertise in the game. My role just kind of evolved into the right hand position from there."

"Word, that's dope ma," Omar said loving the fact that she was a boss and finding it sexy as hell that she called the shots. "But what is a Cocaine Housewife though?"

Sophia laughed, "Sorry, I said that like you knew didn't I? But Cocaine Housewives is the all-female group Santee' started, and it's comprised of the wives and girl-friends of some of his best fallen soldiers. Since he's really big on loyalty, he created the group not only as a way to maintain his own empire, but also as a way to help the widows of his soldiers maintain the lifestyle in which we were all accustomed to. All of the ladies get the exact same plug their men had, and all we're required to do is maintain and cultivate their already existing clienteles."

"Word? That's real shit," Omar said taking in her words. He'd never heard of anything like that before, but he had to admit, it was pretty genius. For a man of Santee's caliber, each one of his men represented millions of dollars of income each month. Losing one of them could be a sizable blow to his pockets. In this game, recruiting new hustlers was no easy task as one had to be very selective of who they let inside their crew. But by replacing his soldiers with their women, Santee' never had to experience a break in his revenue, and it allowed him to remain loyal to his soldiers even in their deaths.

"How long has it been?" Omar asked, wondering if the lost that granted her entrance into the housewives club was still fresh.

"Three years," Sophia replied, looking down into her drink. She didn't offer up any more information than that and Omar could see the sadness in her eyes so he quickly changed the subject.

"Will you be going back to the states soon?"

"Yeah, we should be finishing up here in the next day or two then we'll be headed back to L.A." Sophia replied. She stood up and walked over to the bar to retrieve more ice. Omar couldn't help but to stare at her perfectly shaped ass as she went by. Even though her outfit wasn't revealing, he could still tell that her body was banging underneath it.

"You know, I would really love to see you again once we get back to the states." Omar informed her as she returned to her seat and poured herself another drink. "You should let me take you out sometime."

Omar was officially smitten. Not since the day he met Alaska years ago, had he been so taken by a woman.

Damn Alaska! Omar thought as if he'd just now realized he had a wife. Guilt washed over him because he knew he was wrong for what he was feeling, yet he still couldn't curb the undeniable attraction he felt towards Sophia.

"I'd like that very much," Sophia finally answered after taking a sip of her drink.

"Well then it's a date." Omar smiled, placing his hand on her knee. Her skin was so soft that it caused an instant blood flow to his manhood. He tried to quickly snatch it away, but Sophia grabbed his hand and put it right back.

"It's okay," she smiled seductively. "You can touch me if you like."

The sound of her voice along with the "fuck me daddy" expression on her face was more than Omar could bear. Within seconds his hands were roaming all over her body, and his mouth was covering hers with soft wet kisses. The temperature in the room went up by at least twenty degrees as Sophia began to unbutton and remove her Prada suit jacket. Omar followed her lead, taking off his shirt before gently nudging her to lay her body down onto the couch. He placed his body on top of hers and he began leaving a trail of wet kisses that went from her lips down to her navel.

When he reached the top of her skirt, Omar used his teeth to undo the button and unzip the zipper. He then tugged on the fabric signally Sophia to lift up so that he could get it over her hips. Omar soon learned that she wasn't a big fan of underwear as her pretty shaven pussy slowly came into view. Unable to resist, Omar flicked his tongue across her clit a few times, sampling her sweetness before he stood up and removed the rest of his clothes.

Now it was Sophia's turn to check out the merchandise as Omar's rock hard dick sprung from his boxers. Taking him by surprise, she took his pole into her hands as she opened her mouth and stuck out her tongue, forcing his dick down her throat as far as it would go. Omar's head fell back as he grabbed the sides of her face and moaned out in pleasure. If her head game was this awesome, he was almost afraid to find out what her pussy felt like.

For the next few hours, the two of them hungrily explored the other as each of them filled a need neither of them even realized they had. Their lovemaking was explosive. By the time it was all over, Omar was spent and Sophia had come more times than she could count. They made their way to the bedroom with the sweat still glistening on their bodies; they climbed into the bed and fell asleep in each other's arms.

CHAPTER SEVEN

Sophia

The next morning, sunlight came creeping through the bedroom window much sooner than Sophia would've liked. She was still love drunk from the night before and she just couldn't seem to will her body to move. As she laid there trying to adjust her eyes to the light, Sophia felt around on the nightstand searching for her phone. Peeking through half open eyes, she saw that the time was 9:30 a.m. and she instantly panicked. Omar needed to be back at the airstrip by eight o'clock, and it had been her responsibility to get him there on time. Sophia jumped out of the bed and began searching for her clothes.

"Omar! Wake up baby, we're late." Sophia franticly looked all over the room for her clothes until she finally remembered that they were in the living room. She ran back to the front of the guesthouse and quickly slipped them back on. Using her fingers, she raked her hair up into a messy ponytail, and then she twisted it into a bun which she let rest at the top of her head. Realizing Omar still hadn't gotten up; Sophia went back to the room prepared to physically drag him from the bed if she had to.

"Omar," she shouted, pulling back the covers to reveal an empty bed. *What the hell,* Sophia thought. She was about to head to the master bathroom to make sure he wasn't in the shower when she saw a piece of paper with her name on it lying on the nightstand. In Omar's surprisingly neat handwriting, the note read;

Ma,

    Sorry I didn't wake you. You looked so beautiful and peaceful sleeping that I didn't want to disturb you... But I had to let you know that last night was amazing!! Thank you for allowing me into your world and I'll count the days 'til we meet again. Call me anytime 702-555-5775.

Omar

    Sophia flopped down on the king sized bed and she breathed a bittersweet sigh of relief. On one hand she was happy she wouldn't have to listen to Santee' bitch at her about being late, but on the other she was sad that she didn't get a chance to give Omar a proper goodbye. Flashbacks of his touch invaded her mind as Sophia realized she hadn't felt this way about a man in a long time. It was refreshing yet scary, and she tried to shake the schoolgirl like butterflies that were fluttering in her stomach as she stood up. Grabbing her purse, Sophia headed back over to the main house.

    Sophia quickly showered and got dressed in her favorite red, Dolce and Gabbana suit with matching Louboutin heels. She decided to leave her hair up in the high bun she created earlier; however she did take a brush and some edge control to it in order to smooth it out. Looking like a million bucks, Sophia slid a tube of M.A.C's RiRi Woo lipstick across her lips to finish off her look. She gave herself the once over in the full length bathroom mirror and was pleased with what she saw. She was so pleased in fact, Sophia grabbed her iPhone and snapped a pic, immediately texting it to Omar with the caption,

    My look today is inspired by the fire we made last night :)

Since she knew he was probably still on the plane, she didn't expect an immediate text back. Still, one came through anyway.

Damn ma. You definitely did that. Gorgeous!

Sophia's heart fluttered at his reply. Grabbing her Berkin bag off the bed, Sophia dropped her phone inside the ridiculously expensive purse as she made her way down stairs to the front door. A black on black Cadillac Escalade sat waiting for her with the back door already open and the chauffeur standing beside it.

"Buenos Dias Señora Sophia." He greeted her in his native language, holding out his hand to assist her as she climbed into the back of the truck.

"Buenos Dias," Sophia replied.

The chauffeur closed the door behind her quickly making his way back around to the driver's side. Once he pulled out onto the main road, Sophia gave him the address to where she needed to go. She then leaned her head back onto the headrest, closed her eyes, and prepared herself to complete the task she had initially been sent here to handle.

About an hour later, the Escalade pulled into the parking lot of an old abandon warehouse. The chauffeur parked the truck near the entrance and he assisted her as she got out and went inside.

"Hola gentlemen," Sophia greeted the four men as she walked into the room, her Louboutin heels echoing throughout the empty warehouse announcing her arrival. There was a small table in the center of the room, and each of the men stood up out of respect for her as she walked by taking her seat at the head of it.

"Gentlemen," Sophia said getting right down to the business at hand. "It has been brought to me and Santee's attention that a shipment which was last in your team's possession, has now come up missing. Do any of you know what that means?" Sophia asked as she stood up and slowly began circling the table. She watched each of the men's body language for signs of guilt, and all of them seemed to remain calm except for Miguel, the youngest one. Sophia noticed that he was nervously ringing his hands together as they lay in his lap so she stopped directly in front of him as she continued speaking.

"It means that there is a thief among us my friends. And as you all were told when you accepted your positions, betrayal is never taken lightly within the walls of this organization. Therefore," Sophia paused, signaling for the four goons that were hiding in the shadows of the room to finally step out, "unless one of you can tell me where the shipment is, I have been given orders to kill every last one of you."

The look of fear entered the men's eyes, but still neither of them said a word. Sophia continued to pace the floor, a wicked smile painted on her face as she watched them squirm in their seats. This was her favorite part of the job. Sophia got a rush from playing God and holding another man's life in the palms of her hands. It was the ultimate level of power and she always handled it well.

"Well don't everybody all try to speak at once gentlemen." Sophia smirked. She leaned back against the table using her hands to prop her up, and she crossed her legs at the ankle. She studied the men before her. She knew that no matter what either of them said, today was going to mark the last day of their lives. The only reasons she didn't kill them on sight, was because she still needed to find out the location of the stolen shipment.

"With all due respect, Señora Sophia, my boys and I would never bite the hand that feeds us." Luis, the father to the three others, finally spoke up.

"Is that so?" Sophia asked looking him directly in the eyes. "Then tell me, why is it that Miguel here is dripping sweat all over my warehouse floor?"

Luis looked at his son like he was seeing him for the very first time. He had been so wrapped up in his own thoughts wondering why his entire family had been summoned here, that he never even notice the look of guilt written all over his son's face.

"Miguel," Luis whispered, pain and disappointment dripping from his voice, "Please tell me you had nothing to do with this hijo."

"I… I…," Miguel tried to speak but the fear gripped on to his voice and snatched it out of his throat. Tears welled up in Luis's eyes as he and his two other sons looked on in disgust. Sophia could tell that Luis had no clue of his son's transgressions, and her heart truly went out to him knowing that he still would be killed for them anyway.

"Take the others out back and handle them," Sophia commanded the goons as she removed her jacket and hung it on the back of the chair. "Big Kev and Zoe; y'all stay here with me."

For the next two hours, Sophia sat back as the goons tortured Miguel with everything from cigarette burns to baseball bats. She'd asked him multiple times to give her the location of the shipment, but each time he lied to her. Finally, when Sophia had enough of their twisted little game, she ordered Big Kev to bring in the finale. At five feet tall and weighing in at four hundred and fifty pounds, Big Kev wheeled in the cage of Santee's pet lion Simba. Miguel had been lying unresponsive on the cold warehouse floor, but when he heard the growl of the massive beast, he instantly tried to jump up.

Zoe wasn't having that though, and he placed a heavy hand on Miguel's shoulder forcing him back down. Big Kev came over and he shackled Miguel's ankles together with a chain, and that's when the young Colombian realized his fate. Tears sprung from his eyes as he finally cracked and began telling Sophia everything she wanted to know.

"It's in an old abandon building down by the river!" Miguel shouted. "Three men from the Hernández cartel kidnapped me and made me steal it. They told me if I didn't, they would rape and murder my entire family."

Sophia walked over to Miguel and kneeled down to his level, "Well that's really too bad," she replied with a wicked smile, "Especially seeing as how they're all going to be killed now anyway."

Miguel tried his best to break free as Sophia stood up and signaled for Big Kev to unlatch the cage. With both his arms and feet bound together by the chains, Miguel became a sitting duck as Sophia and her crew casually exited the building.

As she climbed into the back of the waiting Escalade, Sophia could still hear his screams.

CHAPTER EIGHT

Omar

Almost two whole weeks had gone by since Omar returned home from his trip to Colombia, and he hadn't spoken to Sophia once. Although she was calling and texting him non-stop, Omar was riddled with guilt once he got back home and he knew he could never see her again. The night they shared would always be etched into his memory, but Omar's heart belonged to Alaska and he wouldn't risk losing her. As he stepped out of the shower, he heard his phone vibrating on the bathroom vanity and he quickly picked it up. He slid his finger across the screen and a text message appeared:

So it's like that, huh? I let you get a taste of this pussy and you just dip on me with no explanation. Didn't your mother ever tell you not to play with a woman's heart? I guess I'll just have to teach you that lesson.

The text message had Sophia's name above it, and Omar began to shake his head. When they met, Sophia hadn't struck him as the crazy stalker bitch type, but her text messages were becoming increasingly more reckless. Omar knew he had to do something to nip this shit in the bud before Alaska somehow found out. Wiping water from his face with his dry towel, Omar pulled up his contacts and tapped on Sophia's name. Just as he expected, she answered on the first ring.

"Hey baby," she cooed sweetly as if she hadn't just been talking out the side of the neck with craziness in her text message. "I was wondering how long it was going to take you to call."

"Listen, Sophia," Omar said wanting to get straight to the point, "I'm really sorry I haven't gotten back with you, but I need you to stop calling and texting my phone like some fucking madwoman."

"Excuse me," Sophia said surprised by his harsh words. "I think you need to watch your fucking mouth Mr. Drake. Besides, you're the one who told me I could call you anytime."

"Well now I'm telling you that you can't. I know I should have told you this when we were back in Colombia, but I have a wife Sophia. And I can't …"

"A WHAT!?" Sophia cut him off as she completely lost her cool on the other end of the line. "Are you fucking kidding me? So you just used me to get your rocks off while you were away from your wife? Is that it?"

Omar didn't really have the time or energy to sit there and explain to Sophia what should have already been clear. He never intended to use her this way, but he was a man, and sometimes men did stupid things. Still, that didn't change the fact that he was married and that he deeply loved his wife.

"I'm so sorry Sophia, really I am…" Omar didn't know what else to say. "Please don't call or text my phone from here on out."

Omar disconnected the call and shook his head. He was pissed that he had put himself in this position. He hoped it didn't end up affecting his marriage or his partnership with Santee'.

Everything was almost in place and Omar was just about ready to receive his first shipment. Jay and Mo B had taken care of the niggas from the eastside, and they were no longer a problem. Now all Omar needed to do was get off the last of the inventory he had stashed in his warehouse. He wanted to make a clean break from his former supplier, leaving absolutely no strings undone as he moved on to his next venture. After several days of searching, Jay informed him this morning that he'd finally found a buyer who was able to pay cash for all twenty five kilos on such short notice.

After Omar finished getting dressed, he made sure he had his cell phone and his heat, then he headed out the front door on his way to pick up Jay.

✝ ✝ ✝ ✝ ✝

"Man, where the fuck is this nigga?" Omar questioned Jay as the two sat inside of the Charger rolling up a blunt. The two men had been stationed in the parking lot of the 7-eleven on North Las Vegas Boulevard for almost twenty minutes , Big Hank, the nigga they were supposed to be meeting, was still nowhere to be found.

"C'mon O, you know niggas ain't never on time. Just chill out and hit this blunt. That nigga should be here any minute." Jay said reassuringly as he handed the blunt to Omar. Jay was nervous as hell but he was trying his best not to show it. He had vouched for Hank and convinced Omar to go along with this deal even though neither of them knew much about him. This was the first time Omar had entrusted him to bring in new clientele and if anything went wrong, Jay's life could end up on the line. Although they were family, Jay was fully aware that Omar wouldn't hesitate to demote him back down to a corner boy or worse if this meeting proved to be unsuccessful.

"You know, this is exactly why I don't like fucking wit outsiders," Omar said as he put the blunt to his lips, "Niggas don't respect my muthafuckin' time. I'll give dude five more minutes then we rollin' out. I got better shit to do than to sit here waiting on some lame ass nigga." Omar stated as a thick cloud of smoke floated from his lips.

The two men continued smoking in silence as Jay nervously eyed the clock. Four minutes had passed and he was beginning to think that Big Hank was actually going to stand them up. But just as Omar put out the blunt and started up the car, Jay spotted Big Hank's truck speeding into the parking lot.

"Hold up! That's that nigga right there," Jay said pointing to the red Chevrolet Suburban that was pulling into the convenient store's parking lot. Breathing a quick sigh of relief, Jay grabbed the oversized Louie duffel bag from the back seat of the Charger and opened it up. Inside were twenty-five tightly wrapped bricks of pure, un-stepped on Colombian cocaine, as well as, two chrome desert eagles. Jay reached inside and took out the two throwaway pistols, handing one of them over to Omar. He put the other one down in the waistband of his Sean John jeans and opened the car door.

"Lemme go holla at this nigga and make sure everything is straight. I'll be right back," Jay said as he climbed out of the car.

He wanted to make sure Big Hank wasn't on some bullshit before he actually introduced him to Omar. After waiting for him for more than twenty minutes, the last thing Jay needed was for him to be short on the gwap and fuck up the entire transaction.

"Nigga, you don't know how to tell time or some shit? Why the fuck you so late?" Jay grilled Hank as soon as he climbed into the front seat of the truck.

"My bad bro, I had to handle some shit wit my triflin' ass baby moms. Bitch was on some bullshit and locked me out the house so I couldn't get my dough out the safe. I had to kick down the door at my own muthafuckin' crib. Then the crazy bitch had a nerve to pull a fuckin' gun on me," Hank said shaking his head.

Jay looked over at him like he was fuckin' nuts. *If this fat muthafucka can't even control his own bitch, how the hell he think he gonna be running the streets?* Jay thought shaking his head in amazement.

"Yeah, well, no offense my nigga, but that shit sounds like a personal problem. Make sure don't happen again 'cause fam don't appreciate having to wait around on niggas when it comes to business. You feel me?"

"Fo'sho," Big Hank responded knowing he'd fucked up.

"Now, speaking of business, you got that?"

Hank nodded his head and reached underneath his seat retrieving a large black briefcase. When he popped it open, nothing but Franklin faces stared back at the two men.

"It's all here. You wanna count it?"

"Naw, not yet," Jay said eyeing the briefcase. "This store is too fuckin' hot to be conducting any type of business. Follow us over to the spot."

Big Hank nodded his head and Jay hopped out of the truck and headed back over to Omar's car.

"Is everything straight?" Omar asked as he got back inside the car.

"Yeah, everything's cool. I told him to follow us over to the spot on H and McWilliams though. Shit up here is too hot."

"Good call," Omar said as he started up the car and pulled out of the parking lot. It was well after midnight but the city of Las Vegas was just starting to come alive and the traffic was extra thick. Gawking tourist and irritated residents shared the road as everybody and they mama seemed to be out looking for something to get in to.

As they cruised through downtown Las Vegas, Omar puffed on the blunt and bobbed his head to Rick Ross's Teflon Don album. He wasn't really feeling that nigga Hank, but Omar was in a bind and he knew that was the only buyer Jay could find to take the bricks off his hands in such short notice. He only had forty-eight hours to get rid the last of his inventory and pay off his former connect before he picked up his first shipment from Santee'. With the quality of dope Santee' was producing along with his rock bottom prices, Omar was about to make a major come up in the game.

He thought about his wife, Alaska, and how the two of them were going to be the city's most hated couple once he took his rightful place on the throne. Although he was far from a broke nigga, Omar knew teaming up with Santee' was exactly what he needed to take his operation and his paper to the next level. After diligently putting in work on the streets for the past few years, Omar now had a clientele base that stretched all the way from Las Vegas to Detroit and everywhere in between. If he played his cards right, it wouldn't be long before he obliterated his competition and became King.

"I'm about to cause a muthafuckin' blizzard 'round dis bitch," Omar chuckled to himself as he bobbed his head and rapped along with the music. "I think I'm Big Meech/ Larry Hover/ Flippin' work/ Hallelujah..."

They finally arrived at their destination and Omar guided the Charger into the driveway of his westside stash house, shutting off the engine. He waited for Big Hank's truck to pull in behind them before he opened his door and got out. *Showtime*, Omar thought as he tucked the desert eagle discreetly at his side and walked to the front door. Jay and Big Hank trailed slowly behind him. Once they got inside, Omar wasted no time getting down to business.

"Let me see dat cash," he demanded as they all stood inside the semi-empty living room.

"Damn my nigga, you ain't gone even say what's up first?" Hank questioned feeling somewhat offended by Omar's cold demeanor.

"Nigga, I didn't come here to shoot the muthafuckin' shit, I came here to handle business," Omar said dismissing Hank's feelings. "So let me ask you again. What's up wit them racks my nigga?"

Jay got nervous as the two men stood there staring each other down. He placed his hand on his gun just in case Big

Hank got stupid and he was forced to rectify the situation. However, he was relieved when Big Hank finally raised his hands in surrender.

"It's all good my dude. I was just trying to be courteous and shit, "Big Hank replied wearing a smirk. He then put the briefcase on top of a small round table and popped it open. "Like I told yo mans, it's all there but you can count it if you need to."

"Fuck you mean if I need to nigga? I don't need yo muthafuckin' permission." Omar barked, testing Hank's gangsta. He hated doing business with weak ass niggas 'cause they were usually the first ones at the police station whenever some shit went down. If a nigga proved he was able to hold his own, Omar would continue to do business with him. He knew it would be less likely to come back and bite him later on.

"My bad dude, I didn't mean no disrespect." Hank said instantly bitching up.

"That's what the fuck I thought." Omar said as he plugged the first stack of hundred dollar bills into a money counting machine. His instincts told him that Big Hank was a hoe ass nigga before they had even met, but now Omar had conformation. *I can't believe Jay brought this punk ass muthafucka to me,* Omar thought to himself. He made a mental note to holla at him about the situation on the way home.

After ten minutes, the machine had counted and verified every single bill inside the briefcase, totaling four hundred thousand dollars.

"Give him the dope," Omar nodded to his cousin.

Jay quickly removed the bricks from the duffel bag and sat them on the table. He then started to replace them with the bundles of cash. While he waited, Big Hank split open one of the tightly wrapped bricks and dipped his pinky finger into the fine white powder, rubbing it across his gums.

"That's what fuck I'm talking about," Hank said as the potent drug began to numb his gums. He pulled a bag from the bottom of the now empty briefcase and began filling it up with bricks. Once the men finished loading up their respective bags, the three of them shook hands and headed to the front door. Big Hank was walking behind Omar, and Jay was at the rear. Suddenly, Omar got an overwhelming feeling that something wasn't right as he went to open the door. He instinctively reached for the desert eagle Jay gave him just as two huge goons came busting through the door. Before he even realized what was happening, Omar found himself surrounded while staring down the barrel of two .40 caliber pistols.

"Oh, my fault, I forgot to tell you," Big Hank said wearing a huge smile, "You just got GOT my nigga!"

As soon as the words left Hank's mouth, Omar realized they'd fallen for the "okey doke". He tried reaching for his gun again but it was too late. Before he could even grip the pistol's handle, Hank's goons started blazin'. Multiple bullets pierced through Omar's body like a hot knife slicing through butter, and he kicked himself for not listening to his instincts. Him and Jay were completely caught off guard by the ambush and there was nothing either of them could do. As excruciating pain shot through his body, all Omar could think about was Alaska. Her beautiful caramel colored face was the last thing he saw as he collapsed to the floor in a pool of bright red blood. Jay had been hit multiple times as well, and his lifeless body was lying a few feet away from Omar's.

Hank displayed a look of complete satisfaction as he stood and surveyed the gruesome scene before him. When he snatched the duffel bag containing the money from Jay's still tightly clutched hand, Hank felt like David after he beat Goliath with his sling. Omar was about to be the man in Las Vegas and he had been the one to take him down. Hank smiled and tossed the duffel bag over his shoulder. Just as quickly as they came, the three men ran back to Hank's truck and promptly fled the scene.

CHAPTER NINE

Alaska

The sound of the blaring TV awoke Alaska from a much needed nap sometime around midnight. She'd spent the entire day with her sister Montana and her five year old twin nieces, who'd surprised her by coming into town for the weekend. Alaska treated them to shopping and spa treatments along with a trip to Six Flags Magic Mountain. Now she was completely worn out. As she sat up on the side of the bed, she looked around the room and noticed that Omar still hadn't made it home yet. It was unlike him to stay out this late without calling. Alaska checked her cell phone but she didn't see any missed calls. Not wanting to bother him if he was out handling business, Alaska decided to give him an hour before she started blowing up his phone.

By 2:30 in the morning, she'd called and texted him at least a hundred different times, now panic was finally beginning to set in. She decided to call Andraya who now was living back at home with Jay. Alaska knew if he hadn't made it home either, then something was definitely wrong.

"Hello," Andraya answered, picking up the phone on the very first ring.

"Hey girl, it's me," Alaska said trying to sound normal. She could already hear the panic in her home girl's voice and she knew her worst fear had probably come true.

"Oh my God 'Laska, I was just about to call you. I can't get a hold of Jay and I'm really starting to think that something is wrong," Andraya said beginning to cry.

"Calm down Draya," Alaska replied, "I haven't talked to Omar either but I'm sure there must be a good explanation why they haven't called." Alaska wasn't even sure if she believed her own words, but still she put on a brave front for her girl. Between the two of them, Alaska was definitely the stronger one and she always found herself taking the lead in any stressful situation.

"Get dressed. I'm about to come pick you up," Alaska demanded as she grabbed her pink Juicy Couture sweatpants off the floor and slipped them on.

"Where are we going?" Andraya asked still sniffling.

"I'll tell you all that once I get there. Just hurry up and put on some clothes," Alaska said before disconnecting the call.

She threw a white t-shirt over her expensive La Perla bra, and slipped on the only pair of tennis shoes she owned as she grabbed her keys and purse and headed toward the door. Before she could even make it outside, Alaska's cell phone started to ring and Mary J. Blige's voice came blasting threw the speakers. *Like sweet morning dew/ I took one look at you/ and it was plain to see you are my destiny...* Fumbling through her purse to retrieve her phone, Alaska breathed a sigh of relief realizing it was Omar's ringtone.

"Nigga where the hell you been?" she answered, quickly going from scared to pissed off in two seconds flat.

But when she only heard a faint moaning sound on the other end of the line, her heart began to sink for the second time that night.

"Babe, are you alright," Alaska yelled into the phone's receiver trying to figure out what the hell was going on. After a few seconds of dead air, she could finally hear Omar's weakened voice coming through the phone.

"Baby... I'm so sorry," he whispered as Alaska listened to him struggle to speak. "Dat nigga Hank caught us slippin', bay... I don't... I don't think I'm gonna make it."

Alaska could hear the gurgling sound in his lungs as he spoke and she knew it caused by his blood.

"Where are you at?" she asked trying not to show her panic. If he was still able to talk, she figured she might be able to reach him in time enough to take him to a hospital.

"Omar, baby, please just tell me where you are," Alaska repeated when she didn't get an answer the first time.

"I'm at the north side stash house," Omar said before the line went dead.

"Hello! Omar, are you still there? Hello?" Alaska looked down at her phone and saw the call had been disconnected. As she jumped in her Range Rover and headed around the corner to pick up Draya, she called Omar's phone back a thousand times but it just kept going to his voicemail. Hot tears were running down her cheeks as she did damn near 90 down a residential street.

She quickly made it to Draya's house and was glad to see that her girl was already standing outside waiting in the driveway. After Draya jumped in, Alaska high-tailed it to the expressway and then did 110 all the way to the other side of town. Alaska decided not to tell Draya about Omar's phone call in an attempt to keep her calm, but as the two women rode in silence, each one of them feared the worst.

Ten minutes later, Alaska pulled into the driveway of the run down house Omar had taken her to many years ago. Omar's car was in the driveway, and from her truck she could see that the front door was wide open but there didn't appear to be any movement inside.

"What are we doing here," Andraya question with a scared look on her face. She wasn't used to being on this side of town and she reached over to lock her door out of habit.

"I think they might be inside," Alaska said as she took out a chrome .22 that Omar had given her a while back. "Omar called me right before I left, and he told me that they got caught slippin'."

"What! Why didn't you tell me that?" Andraya asked staring down at the gun. "And why the hell didn't you just call the police?"

"Draya, you know the police don't give two fucks about niggas dying in the hood. They would've taken all night to get here, and when they finally did, they would've asked a whole bunch of questions neither of us could answer. Now I need you to just sit tight while I go inside. If you see anything suspicious, just scream, okay?"

Andraya nodded.

She was glad Alaska didn't ask her to go inside with her, because at this point she was completely petrified. Even though she knew her man could be in there dying, Andraya was simply too afraid to go see for herself.

"Please Lord, just let them be okay," Andraya prayed out loud as she kept her eyes glued to the front door. The minute or so that passed since Alaska left and went inside, felt like an eternity to Andraya and she began to wonder if her friend was okay. Just as she built up the courage to climb out of the truck, Alaska appeared in the doorway frantically waving her arms.

"He's still alive! I need your help," she yelled as Draya ran up the driveway. When she reached the door she was shocked to see her girl's once white t-shirt completely covered in blood.

Alaska had made it inside just before Omar took his last breath, and she was able to tell him how much she loved him as she cried and rocked him in her arms. It was only when his faint pulse died out, that Alaska finally released his body and laid him gently on the floor. She kissed his blood-stained lips and closed his eyelids with her fingertips. She removed his chain from around his neck and unclasped his watch from around his wrist. She also took his cell phone out of his hand and retrieved his wallet from his back pocket. Alaska used the bottom of her blood stained shirt to remove his ID from the holder, and she placed it next to his body so he could be identified whenever the police decided to show up. After she took a moment to get herself together, Alaska went over to check on Jay and she found that he was still breathing. She told him to hold on and that everything was going to be alright.

Now, the two petite women were struggling to carry Jay's 220 pound body outside to Alaska's truck. They had to stop and put him down at least three times before they finally got him inside. Although he was unconscious, he was still breathing when Alaska drove off and headed to the hospital. Driving like a bat out of hell, Alaska pulled out her phone and called the police to report that Omar's dead body was still inside the house. She didn't report the victim as a young black male though, instead Alaska told the operator that the victim was a twenty-something year old white female in hopes that the police would get there faster.

As the truck weaved in and out of traffic, Andraya sat in the back seat with Jay crying her eyes out. Although Alaska was devastated, she had completely zoned out knowing there were things she had to do before she would get a chance to just sit down and fall apart. As they pulled into the emergency area of Sunrise Hospital, Alaska began telling Draya what she needed her to do.

"Listen to me Draya," Alaska said locking eyes with her girl in the rearview mirror, "When I pull up to the door, I'm going to call for the nurses so that they can help you take him inside. When they ask you what happened, tell them you don't know anything, and that you found him this way when you went to pick him up from a friend's. Don't give them any other information. Do you understand what I'm saying?" Andraya slowly nodded her head.

"Good." Alaska said as she threw her truck in park and got out screaming for assistance. "Somebody please help us, this man has been shot!"

CHAPTER TEN

One Week Later/Present Day

Alaska awoke from yet another restless night, drenched in sweat and gasping for air. Her heartbeat was racing and her head was still banging from the migraine she developed almost a week ago. She sat upright in the bed as she tried to gain her bearings. Unfortunately for Alaska, this is how she had awakened every morning since Omar's murder. Her frequent dreams about him were keeping her up at night and whenever she did manage to get any sleep, she always woke up like this. As she flung the covers off her body, Alaska glanced at the clock on her nightstand. It was 7:45 in the morning and her alarm would be going off in fifteen minutes. Knowing there was no sense in trying to fall back to sleep, Alaska slowly climbed out of her California king-sized bed and headed to the bathroom.

As she passed by her walk-in closet, Alaska caught a glimpse of the all black Vivian Westwood dress that was hanging on the closet door. Andraya had put it there last night after the two of them decided it was what Alaska would wear to Omar's home-going celebration later this afternoon. Just thinking about the emotionally draining day ahead of her made Alaska want to crawl back into her bed and stay there all day. She hated attending funerals and she definitely wasn't looking forward to having a church full of people all up in her grill asking how she was doing. If it had been left up to her, Alaska would've held a small ceremony with only their closest friends and family. She would've made sure that the people who mattered most got the opportunity to pay their respects, and she would've simply said fuck everyone else. But unfortunately, Omar's mother, Deb, had other plans. She decided her only son should go out with a bang, she felt it necessary to spend fifty thousand dollars on the services, and then invite damn near the entire city to attend them. Since the two of them were just beginning to mend their relationship before Omar was killed, Alaska held her tongue on a lot of things, and she allowed Deb to run the show.

As Alaska splashed cold water on her face, she thought about how drastically her life had changed over the past seven days. She had gone from planning their five year anniversary party, which had been scheduled to take place next weekend, to planning her husband's funeral in just a blink of an eye. Alaska was still in a state of shock and she couldn't completely wrap her mind around the fact that Omar was gone. Sometimes she would sit in her living room and just stare at the front door, praying Omar would somehow miraculously walk through it just one more time. The two of them had been together since Alaska was sixteen and now that he was gone, she felt completely lost. As she grabbed a wash towel from the bathroom cabinet, Alaska had to squeeze her eyes shut and shake her head to stop the visions from that fateful night from replaying in her mind.

Since that day, Alaska's world had been turned upside down. She knew in her heart that nothing would ever be the same, yet she still prayed for the day when her life would return to some degree of normalcy. Although Jay survived the shooting, he had to undergo a lung transplant, while the bullet that struck his spine left him temporarily paralyzed from the waist down. He stayed in the hospital for a few days before being transferred to a long term private rehabilitation center, where he was undergoing rigorous physical therapy and breathing treatments. Alaska, Andraya, and his mother

Diller, were the only people on Jay's visitor's list, and at least one of them came to see him every day.

Alaska cried fresh tears as she removed her toothbrush from its holder. Andraya was supposed to be there any minute to help her get ready for Omar's home going, but all she really wanted to do was climb back into her bed and go to sleep. Finishing up in the bathroom, Alaska grabbed Omar's robe from the back of the bathroom door and put it on. She headed to the kitchen to fix herself some tea.

Just as she put the tea kettle on the stove, Andraya came walking through the door with a grande size cup of Alaska's favorite tea from Starbucks.

"You might as well go ahead and turn that off. I already got you, boo." Andraya sat the tea and her purse on the countertop as she walked over to give her girl a hug.

"How are you feeling this morning?"

"Like shit," Alaska responded as she grabbed the cup of tea and took a sip. "Why can't I just say my goodbyes in private, then bring my black ass back home?"

"Girl, stop with the shenanigans." Draya said frowning at her friend. "I know this is hard, but you have to step in that church today and represent for your husband."

"But, I just don't know if I can handle it," Alaska said as she broke down and more tears began to flow. Andraya hugged her girl tightly, assuring her that everything would be okay as they walked back to Alaska's bedroom to get ready.

Knock, Knock.

"Come in," Alaska said as she sat on the edge of her bed gripping a handful of tissues. Andraya had worked her magic transforming Alaska from a hot ass mess, back into the sleek and pulled together hustler's wife she was made to be.

"Excuse me Mrs. Drake; I just wanted to let you know that the limo has arrived. Whenever you're ready, it'll be waiting for you out front."

"Thank you, Mr. Durant," Alaska replied smiling at the extremely polite funeral director, "I'll be out in just a few minutes."

"Please, take your time," he insisted before softly closing the bedroom door, leaving her alone. Andraya had already left ahead of her so that she could make sure everything at the church was in place. Taking a deep breath, Alaska finally rose from the spot she'd been sitting in for the past hour, and she walked across the room to her full-length mirror. *"Okay, this is it,"* she said while nervously smoothing out the wrinkles in her brand new Vivian Westwood dress. Omar's funeral was scheduled to begin in less than thirty minutes, and Alaska needed to give herself a prep talk before leaving the house. Although she had been crying nonstop since the night he was killed, Alaska knew that today she was going to have to be strong and put on a brave face. She hated anyone to see her emotions. Her father told her when she was just a little girl, that crying was a sign of weakness.

"Just keep your emotions in check and don't let 'em see you sweat," she reminded herself as she stared at her reflection in the mirror. She was sure all of her haters would be in attendance at the funeral, and Alaska refused to give any of them bitches the satisfaction of seeing her breakdown. But even more importantly than that, Alaska had to remain strong for Omar's mother Deb. Although the two of them had just recently begun speaking again, Omar was Deb's only child and she was taking his passing extremely hard.

After touching up her make-up in the mirror, Alaska grabbed her purse off the bed, slipped on her favorite pair of black Louboutin heels, and made her way to the front door. As soon as she stepped outside of her five-thousand square foot home, the rain that had been coming down since earlier this morning seemingly came to a halt and the sun suddenly began to shine. Alaska smiled and blew a kiss up to the sky.

Her heart told her that Omar had something to do with the sudden weather change. He knew how much she hated getting her hair wet and it was just like him to move heaven and earth, or in this case storm clouds, in order to make her happy.

"Right this way Madame," Mr. Durant said as he lightly held onto Alaska's arm, helping her down the steps. "We'll be picking up Ms. Anthony first, and from there we'll make our way on to the church."

Alaska nodded her head in approval as she climbed into the backseat of the waiting limo. As they pulled out of the driveway, Alaska couldn't believe she was on her way to bury the man she'd loved since she was fifteen years old. Her emotions regarding Omar's death had ranged from distraught to anger, with revenge finally weighing heavy on her mind over the last few days.

With Jay out of commission, Alaska was forced to take matters into her own hands when it came to avenging her husband's death. She put the word out to Mo B and a few of Omar's best soldiers, informing them that she was looking for information on Big Hank or any nigga in his crew. So far word on the street was that Big Hank used the money and dope he stole that night to make a come up in the streets of his hometown of Los Angeles. Alaska figured he was probably lying low but she still sent a team out to L.A. to see what they could find. Before they left, she gave each man specific instructions to leave Big Hank alive. If and when they find him, Alaska wanted to make sure her face was the last one he saw as he met his final fate. Alaska smiled at the thought of taking Big Hank out, but quickly put her ideas of revenge aside as she saw they were nearing their destination.

The driver of the limo pulled up to the gate of the newly built sub-division where Omar had recently purchased his mother a house.

"Hola Hector," she said to the short Hispanic man who was always standing guard at the gate, "We're here to pick up

Ms. Anthony for her son's funeral. Can you buzz us in?"

"Si, of course Mrs. Drake," Hector said as he pressed the button to open the gate, "and again, I am so sorry for your lost."

"Thank you, Hector," Alaska replied as the limo slowly passed through the cast iron gate. After directing the driver through the maze of cookie cutter homes, they finally pulled into to Deb's driveway. Alaska waited as Mr. Durant got out and opened her door. As she climbed out of the limo and began to walk up the sidewalk, Alaska could feel her heartbeat start to quicken. She had managed to make it through most of the morning without breaking down, but she knew as soon as she saw the woman who was quickly becoming like a second mother to her, it would become hard to maintain her composure. However, to Alaska's surprise, Deb opened the door with a huge smile on her face and absolutely no tears in sight. She was rocking a killer navy blue suit by Gucci, and her hair and make-up were both laid to perfection. If Alaska didn't know any better, she would have thought Deb was headed to a party, instead of her son's funeral.

"Hey baby," Deb said reaching out to hug Alaska.

As the two women embraced, Alaska damn near passed out from the overpowering stench of liquor that emanated from Deb's body.

"Let me grab my purse out the kitchen and we can go ahead and be on our way." Deb said walking away.

As Alaska watched Deb stumble down the hallway, she wondered if she should be concerned. In the few months since she'd gotten to know her, Alaska could count on one hand how many times she'd seen Deb drink. And even when she did, Deb never consumed more than one glass of wine at a time so Alaska was unsure how well she was able to hold her liquor. As Deb made her way back from retrieving her bag, she stumbled and tripped over her own two feet while walking back down the hallway. Alaska rushed over to help her.

"Mama Anthony, are you drunk?"

"Huh? What are you talking about chile? I ain't drunk," Deb said incredulously as she regained her balance, placing her hands on her hips, "I mean, I had a few shots earlier this morning, but trust me, it's nothing I can't handle. I just needed a little something to take the edge off. You know what I'm saying?"

Alaska nodded. She was disappointed in Deb's behavior, but she totally understood it. While the pain of losing Omar had rocked her to the core, Alaska couldn't begin to imagine what his mother was going through only hours before burying her son.

"Well we better get going, we don't want to be late," Deb said as she began walking towards the front door. As the women passed by the living room, Alaska noticed the half empty bottle of Patron sitting on the coffee table, and it made her smile. *"Well at least she's drinking the good shit,"* Alaska chuckled as they walked out of the door.

After arriving at the church and taking their seats in the front pew, Alaska scanned the enormous crowd looking for any familiar faces. Andraya, Mo B, and Alaska's sister Montana were all there to lend their support, as was all the other friends and family members that were packed inside of the modest church. However, Damon, Omar's childhood friend who resided in Philly, was one of the faces Alaska was most expecting to see but was nowhere in sight. She and Omar had gifted him and his wife with cruise to the Mediterranean as a gift for their anniversary, but they had been due back into the states last night. Still Alaska has yet to hear from him and it was starting to bother her. If D had listened to any of the twenty-something messages she'd left on his phone over the last week, then the first thing he should have done when he touched down was hit her up. Alaska didn't want to tell him that his best friend had been murdered via voicemail. But she made it very clear that it was a code red situation which needed his immediate attention.

"Can you believe I still haven't heard from that nigga Damon yet?" Alaska said to Montana as she came over and took the empty seat next to her on the front pew.

"Really? And why does not surprise me," Montana said twisting up her lips in disgust. "Maybe he did us all a favor and jumped off the fuckin' boat."

"Girl, you so damn crazy," Alaska said laughing at her sister. The mere mention of Damon's name always set Montana off, and Alaska found it amusing. Before Alaska ran off to Las Vegas with Omar, Montana and Damon was a couple for almost five years. Then Montana found out that he had been cheating on her with his now wife, Nona. Brokenhearted, she packed up her shit and left, moving back in with their parents. But to add insult to injury, Montana learned two weeks later that she was pregnant with Damon's child. She ended up having an abortion and ever since then Montana couldn't even stand to be in the same room with him. She ignored his presence whenever he was around.

"I'm just saying," Montana said rolling her eyes, "That would really make my fucking day if he did." Both of the women cracked up laughing. Alaska noticed a few people looking at her funny, but she didn't care.

"You always know just what to say to make me laugh."

"Yeah, well, you know. I do what I can," Montana smiled. "But seriously, you need to stop worrying about Damon's bitch ass and focus on the services."

"Yeah, I guess you're right," Alaska sighed, "It just bothers me that he hasn't called."

"Listen, I don' know what's going on with Damon, and you know the last thing I would ever do is come to his defense, but if there's one thing I know for sure, it's that D loved Omar like a brother. If he had gotten any one of your messages, there's no doubt in my mind that he would've jumped on the first thing smoking to Las Vegas. My guess is that he decided to spend an extra day at sea with his slut bag of a wife." Montana shrugged, "But whatever the case may be, it's not your fucking problem."

Alaska looked at her sister and smiled. She knew Montana was probably right so she decided to let it go. Taking a deep, she finally turned her attention to the front of the church were Omar's casket sat beautifully on display. The top-of-the-line coffin was made from expensive mahogany wood, and it boasted 14kt gold detailing on the hinges and handles. When Deb selected the pricy casket on one of their many visits to the funeral home, Alaska had complained that it was too gaudy and not an accurate representation of Omar's laid back style. But now, under the glowing lights of the church and being surrounded by massive arrangements of flowers, Omar's final resting place seemed to be a perfect fit.

As the ushers closed the doors to the sanctuary, the honorable Pastor Marvin Bivens made his way up to the podium. After asking everyone to bow their heads, the Pastor opened the services with Omar's favorite scripture; Psalm 23; 4-6.

"Ye, though I walk through the valley of the shadow of death, I will fear no evil..."

Alaska began to recite the words along with Pastor Bivens, and the tears she so desperately wanted to keep at bay finally made their grand appearance.

After the services were over and everybody had left the church to head to the cemetery, Alaska found herself still sitting in the front row pew. The funeral director had obliged her request to have a few minutes of alone time with her husband before they carried him away. But now, as Alaska sat staring at Omar's casket, she didn't know quite what to say. After a few minutes she finally stood up from her seat and slowly walked up to the box that would be her husband's final resting place. Tears practically jumped from her eyes as she looked down on him for the first time. The undertaker did a great job making Omar look decent. Still as his body lay there inside the casket, Alaska couldn't help think that he looked nothing like the man she married.

His skin was ice cold to the touch; Alaska had to run her fingers across his face just one more time.

"My love," she whispered as tears dropped onto his white suit. "I promise you with everything that I am and everything that I have; I will find the man who did this to you, and make him pay. Rest up my King, 'cause we shall meet again. And when we do, I hope Heaven has a Four Seasons, because it's gonna be on and poppin'."

Alaska bent down and kissed his lips one last time before softly closing the casket.

When she turned around to exit the church, Alaska was startled by the presence of an older man and a young beautiful woman who were both standing by the exit doors.

"Can I help you," Alaska called out as she tried to place their faces. The gentleman appeared to be of Colombian decent, but Alaska couldn't really make out the female's face because of the black veil that was covering it.

"Are you Alaska Drake," the man asked walking closer.

"Depends on who's asking." Alaska removed her clutch from underneath her arm just in case she needed to reach inside of it and pull out her .22.

"My name is Sebastian Santee', and I come in peace," he replied raising his hands in the air.

Alaska instantly recognized the name as that of the man who Omar had been constantly talking about during his last few weeks. She continued to walk down the aisle way until the three of them met up in the middle and Santee' extended out his hand for her to shake.

"It's very nice to meet you," she said shaking his hand. "And how can I help you?"

"I'm sorry we had to meet under such terrible circumstances," Santee' politely began, "but my associate Sophia and I, just wanted to stop by and pay our condolences. Omar was good man, and I'm terribly sorry for your lost."

"Thank you," Alaska nodded. "Omar spoke a lot about you before he passed. It's nice to finally put a face with the name."

"Likewise," Santee' smiled. "Forgive me as I know this is probably not the time nor the place, but I would really like to speak with you about some unfinished business between Omar and myself."

"Okay," Alaska said somewhat taken aback. "But I'm not sure how much help I'll be to you since I didn't really know much about that side of Omar's life."

"No worries," Santee smiled while handing her a black and gold laminated card that bared his name and phone number. "I know you have to get going, but please just take my card and give me a call whenever you can."

"Okay..." Alaska said hesitantly as she slid the card into her clutch and watched the two of them walk away. The female he was with never even spoke, and Alaska found it strange that the woman was dressed more like the mourning widow than she was. But as she made her way back to the limo, Alaska brushed off the thought.

The rest of the day went by in a fog. Almost twelve hours from the time she left her house that morning, Alaska had finally returned home. She took off her heels at the front door, and by the time she made it back to her bedroom, she had unzipped and removed her dress as well. She was so exhausted she didn't even have the energy to take a shower as she flopped down on the bed and pulled up the covers. She hadn't been able to get much sleep since Omar died, but the second her head hit the down feathered pillow, Alaska was out like a light.

CHAPTER ELEVEN

Sophia

Climbing back into Santee's Maybach, Sophia removed the black veil she was wearing over her face and she placed it in her lap. When Santee informed her that he would be attending Omar's home going, she convinced him to let her go along as well. Even though she was saddened by Omar's death, her main reason for going was just because she wanted to meet the woman who owned Omar's heart. But now that she had, Sophia found herself feeling some kind of way about it. Although she had never been lacking in the self-confidence department, something about Alaska Drake made Sophia feel inferior while she was in her presence, and she didn't like that. She wanted to believe that Alaska was just a frumpy old housewife, but in reality, she was everything Sophia wasn't.

"I hope you're not planning to make her a part of the team," Sophia said to Santee' as she stared out the window.

"As a matter of fact, I was. Do you have a problem with that?"

"As a matter of fact I do," Sophia countered. "She's not built for this life."

"I beg to differ. Besides, she's been a hustler's wife since she was sixteen; I think she may know a little something." Santee' lit his cigar and blew a ring of smoke in Sophia's direction.

"Must you?" she coughed rolling down her window to let in some fresh air. "And you know as well as I do, being a hustler's wife is not the same as actually living the life. They don't do shit but lunch and shop all day fucking day. Hell, that's why half those bitches we got now ain't making no goddamn money. They too busy flossin' and laying up wit the next nigga to actually make any real fucking moves."

Santee' looked at Sophia as if she'd lost her mind. Calmly he blew another ring of smoke into her face before putting his cigar into the ashtray and telling her, "Now, you may be a lot of things chica but the one thing you ain't is me. I say who comes and goes inside this organization so you can go ahead and fall back on this one, okay?"

Sophia didn't even bother to reply. She knew there was nothing left for her to say since she didn't want to tell Santee' the real reason why she didn't want Alaska around. She was just going to have to deal with working alongside Alaska for now until she was able to think of way to get her out. Sophia turned her head and looked out the window as her thoughts drifted to Omar. She missed him and she truly wished things hadn't turned out the way that they did.

"On another note," Santee' said interrupting her thoughts. "Have you talked to your brother lately?"

Sophia frowned. "Yeah, I talked to him yesterday. Why?" Santee' hardly ever asked about her brother and she wondered what the special occasion was.

"Has he checked into the rehab facility yet, or is he still intent on remaining a crack-head?"

"No, he hasn't." Sophia rolled her eyes. She hated the way Santee' looked down on her brother just because he had a problem controlling his addictions. The way Sophia saw it, everybody has a vice; her brother's just happened to be crack cocaine.

"Well, tell him I'm still willing to pay for it whenever he's ready."

"I'll be sure to relay the message," Sophia said sarcastically as she tuned Santee' out.

CHAPTER TWELVE

The next morning, Alaska woke up refreshed and reju-
venated. She was determined not to spend her whole day inside the house, so she quickly got up and showered before
throwing on her favorite BCBG maxi dress. Realizing she
hadn't seen Jay in a few days, Alaska decided to head to the
rehab center to pay him a visit. Although it wasn't her day,
she was sure Andraya and Diller would appreciate the relief.

As Alaska drove to the facility, she couldn't help but
think about the visit she got from Santee' yesterday at
Omar's funeral. His visit had put her on high alert, and she
needed to find out from Jay if the Colombian drug dealer was
going to be a possible threat. Although Santee's seemed polite and sincere, Alaska wasn't trying to have any dealings
with him until she knew exactly what was up.

"Hey guys," Alaska said sounding cheerful as she entered Jay's room. Andraya was sitting at the table going over
some paperwork, while Jay sat up in the bed flicking through
the TV.

"Hey 'Laska," Draya replied as she looked up from the
table. Alaska walked over to Jay's bedside and gave her girl
a hug before leaning over and kissing Jay on his cheek.

"So how's he doing today?" she asked as she sat down
her purse on the table. Jay was unable to speak due to his
lung transplant so Alaska directed her questions to Andraya.
But to her amazement, Jay was the one who answered.

"I'm doing just fine, sis. Thanks for asking," Jay said sporting a huge grin as he allowed Alaska to hear that he had finally regained the use of his voice.

"Oh my God, you got your voice back! That's wonderful news Jay," Alaska said truly happy for her friends. Although she missed Omar like crazy, she didn't have it in her to hate on another couple's happiness; especially Andraya and Jay.

"So does that mean you'll be getting out of here soon?" Alaska asked.

"Naw, I still gotta ways to go in my physical therapy sessions. The doctors said I'll have an 80% chance of walking again if I just stick to the treatments."

"And that's exactly what he's going to do," Andraya said as she stood up and gave Jay a kiss. Even though the two of them were still working through their issues, Draya had been right by his side every day since the shooting. She hadn't quite come to terms with the fact that he was having a baby, but she still held him down.

"Will you be here for a while 'Laska? It's been an eventful day and I think I'm gonna get outta here and head home so that I can get some rest."

"Girl, boo." Alaska said waving her hand dismissively. "You know I got you. Gone on and get out of here so you can get some rest."

"Thanks girl. I'll be back in a few hours, okay baby?"

"Chile' he's fine," Alaska said pushing Draya towards the door. "Take yo ass home and get some sleep 'cause them big ass bags you sportin' under your eyes is not the hotness."

The three of them cracked up laughing and Andraya playfully hit her friend on the arm. "Whateva heffa,"

After she gathered her things, Draya kissed Jay one more time and she gave Alaska a hug. "I'll see y'all in a little while."

As she walked out the door, Jay turned his head away from the fuzzy, 19" TV he had been watching, redirecting his attention to Alaska. "So how have you been holding up sis?"

"I'm well," Alaska replied taking a deep breath. "The services went off without a hitch yesterday, and everything turned out beautifully."

"Good." Jay nodded, still upset that he couldn't be there. "I know my nigga is in Heaven now resting up."

"Indeed. And guess who showed up at the end of the services?"

"Who dat?"

"Sebastian Santee'."

"Word?" Jay asked as he pushed a button on controller to elevate the head of his bed. "What did he want?"

"I'm not really sure. I was actually hoping you could answer that. He gave me his card and told me he wanted to speak with me about some unfinished business between him and Omar."

Jay's mind began to race as he tried to think of a reason why Santee' would've went to see Alaska.

"I think Omar may have owed him some money," Jay lied trying to keep Alaska from co-mingling with Santee'. He didn't know what the nigga had up his sleeve, but whatever it was he didn't want Alaska involved. "Why don't you leave me his number and I'll call him a little later and see what's up."

"Alright," Alaska agreed digging in her purse for the card. "Shit, I forgot I changed purses. I'll text it to you when I get back home."

"Cool," Jay responded before quickly changing the subject. "So what's up with your finances? Are you okay? You need me to tell Draya to lace you wit a little dough?"

"Naw, things are getting a little tight but I'll manage. You know Omar always planned for a raining day, so he left me with a pretty hefty sized emergency fund. Plus, I still

HEAVY

have the revenue coming in from the online store. Now I just gotta figure out how to budget the shit," Alaska laughed.

She sat and kickin' it with Jay until the evening nurse came in to administer his medicine a few hours later. Once the medication made its way through Jay's system, he quickly drifted off to sleep and Alaska left him alone to rest.

Alaska ran a few errands after leaving the rehab center and she finally made it back home a few hours later. As she pulled her truck into the garage, her mind was still subconsciously replaying Santee's visit. When she went inside the house, the first thing Alaska did was retrieve Santee's card from her clutch, and then she grab her cell phone. Curiosity was killing her. Although Jay said he would call, Alaska decided she was a big enough girl and could do it herself.

Sitting there with the phone clutched in her hand, Alaska was trying to recall if she had ever heard Omar speak negatively about Santee' in any way. When her memory bank came up empty, she swiped her finger across the screen to unlock her phone, then she typed in Santee' number. Common sense was telling her that if Omar really did owe this man some money, the worst thing she could do was avoid him. He was a very powerful man and whether she called him back or not, he could still reach out and have her touched whenever he wanted. Alaska took a deep breath before pressing the talk button and waited for Santee' to answer the phone.

"Hello." he answered, his deep baritone voice vibrating the phone's speakers. Alaska momentarily lost her voice out of fear, and she had to swallow the lump lodged inside her throat before she was able to speak.

"Hi umm... is this Mr. Santee'?" Alaska asked nervously.

"Yes it is. Who's speaking?"

"Umm, yeah... this is Alaska Drake, Omar Drake's wife."

"Ahh, yes. The lovey Mrs. Alaska Drake. It's so good to hear from you," Santee' said as if he hadn't asked her to call. "How are you doing today?"

"Very well, thank you. I had a small break in my schedule so I thought to go ahead and give you a call." Alaska replied. She really wanted to just come out and ask him what the hell he wanted, but she didn't want to be rude.

"I see. Well I don't want to keep you so let me get straight to the point."

Thank God, Alaska thought as she listened intently to what he had to say.

"Before your husband died, we had big plans in the works that was going to make both of us a lot of money. But now, since he's gone, there's a huge void in my business and I was hoping you could fill it."

"Wait, are you asking me to step in and fill his shoes?" Alaska asked incredulously. "I've never sold dope; I'm just a housewife for God sakes."

"I totally understand your hesitation," Santee' chuckled. "Listen, how about we meet tomorrow for dinner? I can explain things much better in person. You can meet me at SW Steakhouse inside the Wynn Hotel, and that way we can enjoy a nice meal while we go over the details."

Alaska was leery but she agreed to meet Santee' anyway. After they agreed upon a time, she hung up the phone and headed to the bathroom. She immediately walked over to the whirlpool bathtub and turned it on. Setting the water to a comfortable seventy-eight degree temperature, she dropped in a capful of lavender and calamine bath salts. The calming aroma of the bath products helped to relax Alaska's mind, and she could feel the tension leaving her body as she took off her clothes and climbed inside the steaming hot tub.

As she gently lowered her body into the hot water, Alaska wondered if she could actually pull off being a drug dealer. Although she had watched Omar do it for years, it was a whole different ballgame when she thought of doing it herself. But as Alaska thought about the growing stack of bills that were continually filling up her mailbox every day, she realized that taking Santee' up on his offer may be her only option.

CHAPTER THIRTEEN

Andraya

Draya walked into Maxie's Lounge located on the outskirts of the city, and she took her regular seat at the bar. Ever since the shooting, this had been the one place where she could come to chill out and clear her head. So much had gone down in the last few months that at times she felt like she was spinning out of control. With Jay disabled and their financial future uncertain, Draya had fallen back on the only thing she felt would help her cope; liquor. A former alcoholic with more than two years sober, she felt hella guilty for falling off the wagon yet again. Jay and Alaska had already supported her through one stint in rehab, and she didn't know if they had it in them to weather that storm with her again, so she took extra precautions to make sure neither of them found out.

"Hey beautiful," Sam, Draya's favorite bartender, greeted her as she sat down.

"Hey, Sam" Draya smiled as she slid onto the buttersoft, leather barstool. "Gimme the usual."

"One long island ice tea and two double shots of Patron; coming right up!"

As she waited for her drinks, Andraya wished for the millionth time that things on the night of the shooting had turned out differently. She knew it was crazy, but a small part of her wondered if her life would be less chaotic now had Jay died that night too. At least that way she wouldn't have to deal with the guilt she felt every time she saw him.

HEAVY

Although they'd been together for many years, Draya's feelings for Jay were slowly starting to change. When they first met, Draya was a fifteen year old runaway and Jay was her eighteen year old knight and shining armor. He rescued her from a life on the streets and replaced it with one of comfort and luxury. Back then, Jay was just one of the many corner boys working in Omar's crew. While he wasn't quite 'ballin' out the gym, he made enough money to keep up their hood rich appearances. As his girl, Draya stayed laced in the finest gear, rocking the hottest shoes and carrying the flyest purses, all while pushing the newest whips. Her days were spent shopping, going out to eat and hanging with her friends. Jay gave her a life that once upon a time she could have only dreamed of. He was good to her and he always stood by her side even when she seemed determined to fuck things up. But, with all that being said, Jay still had one major character flaw that Draya couldn't get over; his compulsive cheating.

Now, at a time when she knew he needed her most, Draya was beginning to question the extent of her own loyalty, and part of the reason had to do with the baby he had on the way. While she still loved Jay and would always be grateful for the way he changed her life, his impending fatherhood, as well as his grim prognosis since the shooting, left Draya on edge and honestly she was scared shitless. All of the surgeries, hours of physical therapy and talks of him possibly never being able to walk again made Draya realize everything she had could be gone in a blink of an eye. She felt guilty for thinking it, but if Jay was disabled and could no longer give her the lifestyle she had grown accustomed to, she wasn't sure if she would be able to stick around. Draya's biggest fear was being broke and she would do just about anything to avoid it.

"Here you go pretty lady." Sam said interrupting her thoughts as he placed her drinks on the bar in front of her. "Let me know if you need anything else."

"Thanks, love."

Andraya immediately grabbed one of the shot glasses and tossed the clear liquid to the back of her throat. She then picked up the second glass and did the same. Just as she was about to go in on her Long Island, Draya got the feeling that somebody was watching her. She swiveled the barstool around and scanned the crowd. When she realized nobody was paying her any attention, she figured she was just being paranoid.

But then she saw him.

Standing six feet tall with skin as black as night, Draya's heart began to race as she locked eyes with a demon from her past. His name was Xavier Thomas, and he was the reason she was forced to run away from home all those years ago. He was her older sister's boyfriend and more than five years her senior, but that still didn't stop the two of them from messing around. Their flirtations started out innocent at first. Whenever he was around Draya would wear the skimpiest clothes she could find in order to accentuate her already overdeveloped curves. And Xavier would feel on her ass and whisper freaky things in her ear whenever her sister wasn't looking. It wasn't long before their relationship turned physical. One day, when her sister left the two of them alone to go pick up a pizza, Xavier seized the opportunity to finally get a taste of what Andraya was working with. He knew they didn't have enough time to fuck, so he decided to just eat her pussy instead.

From the moment his tongue slid across her clit, Andraya was turned out. She had let an ex-boyfriend finger her one time before at the movies, but Xavier was doing things to her that she'd only seen in pornos. From then on, Andraya let him get a taste of her cookie every chance she got. It wasn't long before she finally let him take her virginity, and when he did her nose was open wider than ever before. Draya was in love and her naïve young mind believed Xavier was too. At fifteen when she became pregnant with his child, Draya thought for sure he would dump her sister and finally make her his girl. Instead, he gave Draya her very first lesson in heartbreak.

When she told Xavier she was pregnant he tossed her five hundred dollars and told her to get an abortion. He was so scared of facing statutory rape charges for having sex with a minor that he up and left town a few days later. Then, to add insult to injury, when Draya finally told her family the news, her sister beat her ass like she was a bum in the street, and her mother promptly kicked her out of the house for disgracing the family. It didn't matter that Draya suffered a miscarriage as a result of the beat down her sister gave her. The damage to their relationship was already done, and Draya knew she could never go back home.

Flash forward to this very moment and Draya could still feel the same sense of loneliness and abandonment she felt all those years ago as she stared into his eyes. Frozen in her memories, Draya was unable to move as she watched Xavier make his way over to the bar. Every part of her brain was telling her to grab her shit and run, but something inside her heart was beckoning her to stay.

"Little Andraya Harper," he sang calling her by her maiden name. He walked over and stood in front of her. "Damn ma, I ain't seen you in forever."

Xavier leaned in to kiss her cheek and surprisingly, Draya didn't feel the urge to stop him. She welcomed the softness of his lips against her skin and she shivered as the smell of his cologne brought back memories of his impeccable dick game.

"I'm not *little* Andraya anymore. In case you didn't notice, I'm a grown ass woman now." Andraya turned her back to him and proceeded to finish her drink.

"You damn sho' right about that." Xavier admired her curves as he sat down on the stool next to her and ordered a drink of his own, "You want anything, ma?"

"Give me another double shot of Patron."

As Sam went off to get their drinks Andraya played with the tiny umbrella that was perched on the rim of her glass unsure of what to say next. Xavier's presence sent her heart on an emotional rollercoaster and she couldn't to think straight. After years of wondering how she would react if she ever saw him again, Draya was shocked at the level of her calmness. Their relationship, albeit a short one, had altered the course of her life and at one point in time she hated him for that. But now, as she sat next to him for the first time in more than six years, the only thing she felt was an undeniable urge to ride his dick. Maybe it was the alcohol, or maybe it was just his swag. Either way, Draya was definitely ready to relieve some stress.

"So," Xavier said as he handed Sam a credit card to pay for their drinks, "I guess I owe you an apology, huh?"

"An apology," she replied nonchalantly as she sipped on her drink, "What for?" Draya was pretending to be clueless in order to disguise the fact that she had been waiting years just to hear him say those words.

"C'mon ma, don't front," Xavier said calling her out. "I know you're probably still pissed at me for the fucked up way I handled our situation back in the day."

Draya waived her hand dismissively. "Nigga please, that was ten damn years ago. Believe me when I tell you, I'm sooo over it."

Xavier smiled. He could tell from her body language that she wasn't telling the truth but he decided to leave it alone.

"Well even if you are over it, I still want to apologize. I talked to your sister for the first time a few months ago and she told me everything that went down after I left. It fucked me up to hear what you went through just because I was too scared to man up to my actions. So I promised myself if I ever saw you again I would apologize."

"Well," Draya asked unmoved by his spiel, "Are you done?"

Xavier smiled and shook his head. She was trying to play hard and it was turning him on.

"Yeah ma, I'm finished."

"Good," Draya said as she grabbed her brand new Michael Kors bag from the stool next to her and stood up. "Let's go back to my place then."

CHAPTER FOURTEEN

Alaska woke up on the day of her meeting with Santee'
feeling energized. She got up early, dressed, and left the
house planning to spend the entire day getting ready. She
wanted to make sure she looked presentable so she made ap-
pointments to get her hair, nails and toes done at a salon near
the hotel. She even scheduled a thirty minute mini-massage
at the spa inside the Wynn so she that she would appear more
relaxed during their meeting.

After Alaska finished up at the salon, she still had more
than two hours to kill before she headed over to the restaurant. She decided to hit up the Forum Shops at Caesars Palace to see if they had anything good. Even though she already had a dress for the evening, she figured it wouldn't
hurt to have a few different options. Alaska drove her truck
up to the hotel's valet and waited for the attendant to open
her door. After she grabbed her expensive Berkin handbag
she climbed out of her truck and handed the attendant a
twenty dollar tip. As she made her way inside the building,
the heels of her stilettos clicked loudly across the pavement.

For the first time in a long time, Alaska was starting to
feel like her old self again as she strutted through the mall
like a diva. The Diane von Furstenberg wrap dress she was
wearing hugged every inch of her voluptuous frame, and
Alaska could feel niggas checking her out as she walked by.
Gwen, the backup hairstylist she used, had whipped Alaska's
chestnut brown locks into beautiful cascading curls that

flowed endlessly down her back. Her caramel, sun-kissed skin was glowing without even the slightest hint of make-up, and Alaska was sure she looked as good as she felt.

As she walked into the Dolce & Gabbana store, she debated calling Andraya to let her know about the meeting. She knew telling her girl probably wasn't the best idea since Draya couldn't hold water and would promptly relay the information directly to Jay. But Alaska also knew that it wasn't wise to meet up with a man like Santee' and not inform anybody of her whereabouts. If something was to pop off, she wanted her people to know exactly where to start looking.

Still, Alaska opted to throw caution to the wind as she continued browsing the clothing racks. After their conversation last night, her instincts were telling her that Santee' was on the up and up, and that she didn't need to be afraid of him. So for right now, Alaska decided to keep her contact with him a secret until she felt Jay and Draya needed to know about it.

Alaska checked out a few more stores before leaving out of the mall empty handed. She retrieved the valet ticket stub from her purse and gave it to the attendant. As she stood there waiting for him to return with her truck, Alaska noticed a red Suburban pull into the lot. The bass coming from inside the SUV was so loud it rattled every window in the near vicinity. The rims on the truck's 24" inch tires were so shiny that Alaska had to shield her eyes in order to look directly at them. She wondered who was inside the Suburban and something was telling her she needed to stick around to find out. But after the valet brought back her truck, Alaska realized she didn't have time to sit around and wait. She needed to be at the Wynn in fifteen minutes so she hopped inside her truck and took off.

Alaska arrived at the Wynn Hotel and Casino looking like a million bucks. She dabbed a small amount of nude MAC lip gloss across her full lips, as she made sure every curl on her head was still in place. Rocking a pair of True

Religion high-waist dark denim jeans, along with a cream and gold bustier that she got from the Gucci, Alaska looked like she belonged on somebody's runway. She loved the way the bustier exposed her sexy neckline and feminine shoulders, and she purposely opted not to wear a necklace in order to show them off. Alaska topped off her look with a pair of sparkling gold $2,000 red bottom heels, and a gold Louie Vuitton handbag.

"Good evening Madame," the maître d greeted her as she walked through the entrance. "Do you have a scheduled reservation tonight?"

"Yes. I believe it's under the name Santee'," Alaska replied.

"Of course," the maître d said with excitement. "Right this way Madame. Señor Santee' has been anxiously awaiting your arrival."

Alaska followed the middle aged white man through the restaurant until they reached the outside terrace where Santee' was waiting.

"Your guest has arrived Señor," he said as he stepped aside to present Alaska.

"Gracias Jeffery. Can you have Tracy bring up a chilled bottle of Krug Rosé, please?"

Jeffery simply nodded then disappeared to fulfill Santee's request.

"My darling Alaska, it is a pleasure to see you again." Santee' said softly kissing the back of her hand, "You look absolutely gorgeous this evening. Please, come have a seat," he smiled as he pulled out her chair.

"Thank you," Alaska said as she sat down. She was lightweight taken aback by how handsome Santee' was. When they met at Omar's homegoing, Alaska's mind was all over the place and she hadn't realized how attractive he was until now. She could feel butterflies forming in the pit of her stomach.

Girl, this is not a date, Alaska silently tried to remind herself, *you're here strictly to handle business.*

Their waitress Tracy brought back the requested champagne and then she took their orders. Nervous, Alaska practically downed the contents of her glass in one gulp.

"Whoa! You better be careful there little lady. That stuff will sneak up on you," Santee' warned. He needed her to have a clear head when they got down to business so he tried to prevent her from getting wasted.

"Yeah, you're right," Alaska said putting the empty glass back down on the table, "I guess I was just a little thirsty."

"It's okay darling. But if you don't mind, I'd like to get down to business before our food arrives. That way we can sit back and relax while we enjoy our meals."

"Works for me," Alaska replied reaching into the breadbasket to remove a roll.

"So as I stated to you over the phone, Omar and I were on the brink of a very lucrative business venture before he passed. And since he's no longer here to help me bring that plan to fruition, I've decided to go another route. However, I need the addition of an intelligent, beautiful, and fearless woman in order for it to do it."

"And you think that woman could be me?" Alaska questioned.

"Yes, I do," Santee' answered.

Alaska broke off a small piece of her roll and placed it in her mouth. She still wasn't exactly sure what Santee' was asking, but she was intrigued enough to continue listening as he further explained.

"As you may know, I work with many dealers throughout this country. Most of them are just mid-level hustlers. But every now and then I get that special one that has what I like to call "kingpin potential". When that happens, I try to do everything I can to help them reach that elevated status. But as we all know, success in this game can be fleeting, and often times it's downright elusive. Just like Omar, many of my protégés either get killed out in the field, or they end up behind bars. This leaves many beautiful women, just like yourself, alone and struggling.

"So, as a way to help some of those women out, I created a small group comprised of the wives, fiancés and girlfriends of some of my best men. Currently, there are fourteen woman spread across the country that have taken me up on my offer and stepped in to fill the shoes of their men. I would like to offer the same thing to you," Santee' finished, taking a sip of his champagne.

"I see," Alaska responded. She was contemplating everything Santee' just said but she was still unsure.

"You do know that I've never conducted a drug deal a day in my life right? I mean I watched Omar do it for years, and I even rode shotgun with him on a run or two, but I'm not sure I'm cut out for that life."

"And you don't have to be. You'll simply act as middleman between me and Omar's already extensive clientele. When someone calls to re-up, you relay the order to me and I'll dispatch one of my soldiers to make the actual delivery. It's just that simple."

Alaska sat back and wondered why the hell Santee' didn't just explain it that way in the first place. As long as she didn't have to touch any product, Alaska was ready to get shit poppin' as early as tonight. Since she still had Omar's old cell phone, all she had to do was hit up all his contacts and let them know she was taking over.

"So how much money will I be making?" Alaska asked as the waitress finally arrived with their dinners. Santee' waited until Tracy finished serving their food and refilling their drinks before he answered Alaska's question.

"Well you know how a typical transaction normally works right?" Santee' asked attempting to figure out just how far he needed to break things down.

"Of course I do," Alaska said remembering everything that Omar had taught her over the years.

"Great!" Santee' smiled. "Your price would be $15,500 per brick. In today's market you can resell a kilo for much as $25,000, depending on whom and where your customer is. On average, you could be making anywhere from a couple hundred thousand, to a few million dollars every month depending on how much you're able to move."

"I'm in," Alaska's mouth said before her brain even realized it. Although it might've been the liquid courage taking over her mind, Alaska was feeling like she might actually be able to pull this off.

"Perfect, then it's settled," Santee' declared as he took the first bite of his filet mignon. "And if you're free after dinner, I'd like to take you to meet some of the other ladies. Or should I say, the other housewives?" he chuckled.

"Housewives?" Alaska said in bewilderment.

"Yeah, the ladies have dubbed themselves the Cocaine Housewives of Las Vegas" Santee' explained.

Alaska smiled as she dug into her plate, "Ha! I absolutely love that name." Feeling like she'd made the right decision by joining the team, Alaska breathed a sigh of relief as she sat back and enjoyed her meal. Now she didn't have to worry about being frugal with the last of her savings, and she would also be in a better position to avenge Omar's death. As far as Alaska was concerned, hooking up with Santee' was a win-win situation.

After Alaska and Santee' finished their dinner, the two of them headed upstairs to the penthouse suite were the rest of the ladies were waiting. As Alaska fixed her hair and reapplied her lip gloss in the elevator's mirrors, she wondered if she'd get along with the other women. Aside from Andraya and her beautician Jackie, Alaska didn't have very many female friends. She didn't have time for the backstabbing and cattiness that usually ran rampant throughout cliques of women.

As they reached the door of the high-rise suite, Alaska could hear the ladies talking and laughing on the other side. She tried her best to ear hustle and see if their conversation had anything to do with her, but she couldn't make out any of what they were saying through the thick wooden door. She put her guard up and prepared herself for a lukewarm reception at best. Santee' opened the door and she slowly strolled into the beautifully decorated suite. He led the way to the sitting room where the four other women were chilling on a huge couch.

"Hey ladies, I'm back," Santee' announced. All of them instantly redirected their attention to Alaska as Santee' began the introductions. "Alaska, this is Daphne, that's Sophia, and over there is Kim and Ta'Kiyha."

"Hey!" the group said in unison.

"What's up everybody," Alaska replied slightly letting her guard down.

"You want a glass of champagne?" asked Sophia, the woman Alaska recognized from Omar's service.

"Sure, why not?"

Alaska kicked it in Santee's suite getting to know the other ladies until 3 o'clock the next morning. When she was finally ready to go home, Santee' called her a cab. She was clearly too tipsy to be driving. After she made it home and took a quick shower, Alaska climbed into her California king-sized bed thinking about all the money she was about to be making. But even more rewarding than the bread, was the fact that Alaska was now one step closer to avenging Omar's death. Realizing she had to be smart about her plan of attack, she decided she would to use her connection with Santee' as a way to get closer to Big Hank. The money and dope he stole from Omar should have helped him to become a major player in the game, so Alaska knew it was only a matter of time before they ran into each other. And when that time came, Alaska promised that the situation wouldn't end so sweet for that muthafucka.

After she said her prayers and before she drifted off to sleep, Alaska grabbed the picture of her and Omar off the nightstand and she placed her lips against it before laying it in the bed beside her.

CHAPTER FIFTEEN

Three soft knocks on his room door awoke Jay from a much needed nap. The light from the hallway illuminated the dark room as his visitor opened the door and stepped inside. Even in the darkness, Jay was able to make out her perfect silhouette and his dick got rock hard instantly. Without saying a word, she slowly made her way to Jay's bedside while seductively removing all her clothing along the way. She stood there naked as the day she was born, and Jay began to stroke his dick as he admired her incredible body.

"It's time for your medicine," she cooed as she climbed in the small twin sized hospital bed and got on top of him. Sliding down between his legs, she gripped his dick with her right hand and cupped his balls with her left. As her soft hands expertly messaged his dick and balls; Jay closed his eyes in anticipation for what was to come. He had never met a woman who could suck a dick as good as she could. The sensation of her soft lips moving up and down on his shaft, accompanied by the extreme warmth and wetness of her mouth always drove Jay wild and today was no different. A small moan escaped his lips as she took his dick and slid all nine inches down her throat.

"Aww shit," Jay said as she used her throat muscles to squeeze his dick. Her mouth felt like a pussy and he gripped the sides of the bed 'cause it was all he could do to keep from cuming.

"Mmm ...You like that daddy?" She asked, looking him directly in his eyes.

"Yeah, ma, that shit feels so fucking great."

Jay placed his hand on the back of her head as he guided his tool back down her throat. After she sucked him off for a few more minutes, Jay motioned for her to climb on top of him. Since he hadn't regained full use of his legs yet, they usually only did it in one position, but today Jay was dying to hit that ass from the back. As she reached over him to grab a condom from the nightstand, Jay flicked his tongue over her nipple and she giggled.

"That tickles," she said as she opened the condom and slid it over his dick using only her mouth.

"Turn around," Jay commanded. "I want you to ride this dick backwards so I can see that ass." Without protest, she complied with Jay's request and did exactly as he asked. She knew Jay was an ass man, and since she definitely had more ass than the average chick, she had no problem letting him see what she was working wit. Placing his hands on her hips, Jay watched as his dick disappeared between her caramel colored ass cheeks and then reappeared as she expertly bounced up and down.

"Yea, right there, ma." Jay said smacking her ass until it turned red. "Bounce that ass for Daddy."

She moved her body like a pro, grinding her hips and contracting her pussy muscles all while making her ass clap. Although Jay tried his best to hold back the explosion building in his groan, it wasn't long before he lost the battle.

"Aww, shit. I'm 'bout to cum, ma." She immediately jumped off his magic stick and turned her body around to face him. Right as his nut reached the tip of his dick, she covered it with her warmth of the mouth and Jay almost lost control as he shot his frustrations down her throat.

"Damn baby, you did that shit," Jay said as he watched her pick up her scrubs from the floor. Smiling, she winked her eye at him as she walked into the tiny bathroom to clean herself up. Nurse Sharonda Fatty was Jay's latest conquest. From the moment she checked him into the facility, Jay knew he had to have her. Her dark chocolate skin, fat ass and 28" Brazilian weave, made her resemble a thicker version of singer Kelly Rolland.

"I got those items you asked for," she called out from the bathroom.

"Oh word? Good lookin' out ma."

"No problem. Just make sure you keep it between me and you. If anybody found out I brought this stuff in here, I could lose my job," she said emerging from the bathroom rocking a pair of purple hospital scrubs.

"Don't even trip. You know I got chu ma."

Nurse Fatty handed Jay a bag with the three items he requested; a throwaway cell phone, a quarter bag of kush and a pack of White Owl cigarillos. Even in the hospital, paralyzed from the waist down, Jay was still up to his old tricks.

"You know you really shouldn't be fucking wit that shit, right?" Nurse Fatty said as she swung her handbag over her shoulder. "I would hate to see you fuck around and end up right back on that operating table fighting for your life, all 'cause you had to get high."

"Aww 'cmon, ma. After that fire ass pussy you just served up, now you gonna turn 'round and ruin it by naggin' a nigga?" Jay smacked her on the ass to let her know his comment was all in fun.

"I'm just sayin'. You ain't gonna be able to enjoy this pussy if you pushing up daisies, nigga."

"You right about that," Jay chuckled as he held the bag of kush up to his nose and took a sniff. "But seriously, I really appreciate you bringing this stuff in for me especially the phone. I got some business I gotta handle and I can't do that shit from any of the phones here."

"It's no problem," Nurse Fatty replied with a smile. "Listen, I gotta go clock in for my shift, but I'll be back on my break to take you out to the terrace. No one should be out there at that time so you'll be able to smoke then. Now make sure you put that shit up before somebody else comes in and sees it."

"Alright," Jay said as he stuck the bag of weed underneath his pillow. "I'll holla at you later."

Nurse Fatty checked her reflection in the mirror one last time then she headed out the door. Once she was gone, Jay immediately grabbed the cell phone and hit the power button. It was almost two o'clock in the morning but the call he was about to make couldn't wait another minute. Lying in his room night after night for more than a month forced Jay to think about his future once he was finally released. Although he had stacked up more one hundred and fifty thousand before the shooting, he knew that amount was quickly dwindling since Draya had been using large chunks of it to help cover their monthly bills.

Before Omar was killed, Jay was content with being second in command. He understood that once you became the man and made it to the top, the only other place to go from there was the bottom so he found his comfort zone somewhere in between. While others had aspirations of becoming King, Jay knew his position and he played it well. As Omar's right hand, Jay was privy to every aspect of the business expect for one; Omar's connect. Aside from knowing their names, Jay never dealt with that side of the business. So when Alaska called him this morning and told him about her meeting with Santee', Jay realized the keys to the game had literally just fallen into his lap. With Alaska still connected to Santee', it wouldn't be long at all before he was back on his feet.

Punching in the phone number, Jay put the cell phone on speaker and waited. After two rings, a familiar male voice answered the phone.

"Talk to me."

"My nigga Mo B," Jay replied, excited to hear his best friend's voice. "What the fuck is good wit chu fam?!"

"Shit, I can't call it," he said nonchalantly, "who dis?"

"Nigga, I ain't been gone that damn long. Who the fuck it sound like?"

"Jay!" Mo B exclaimed, unable to believe his ears. After weeks with no word, he just assumed the rumors about his boy getting murked during the robbery were true. Now he realized he should've known better. "Nigga, where the fuck you been? I thought you were dead or some shit."

Jay chuckled. He knew the streets had been talking and speculating on the reason for his disappearance. Since the day he checked into the hospital the only people he had contact with were Draya, Alaska, and his mother. Fearing that Hank and his crew would try to finish the job, Draya checked him into both the hospital and the rehab center under an assumed name. So Jay knew he couldn't fault his best friend for thinking the worst.

"Man, I just had to lay low for a minute, you feel me? I took a few hits during the robbery and I'm just now bouncing back."

"Word," Mo B replied, happy to hear his boy was alright. "You know the streets been talking real grimy since you disappeared though right. Niggas runnin' around town speculating all kinds of crazy shit."

"Like what," Jay quizzed.

"Muthafuckas saying you were the one behind the set up. They claim once you got your cut of the dough, you skipped town and went into hiding. Others are sayin' you got murked but the police can't find the body."

Jay shook his head. He knew the streets would be talking in his absence, but it still amazed him how niggas took rumors and just ran with the shit. It didn't make him any difference though. The fact that people thought he was either dead or on the run actually worked in his favor. If everybody thought he was ghost already, then they'd never see him coming when he made his return.

"That's the word, huh?" Jay chuckled. "Well Imma show niggas what's up real soon. Until then, let them muthafuckas continue to believe whatever they want. You feel me?"

"Fo' sho my nigga, your secret's safe with me."

Mo B took a hit of his blunt and momentarily held the smoke inside his lungs before slowly blowing it out. Jay didn't speak on the rumors pointing to his involvement in the set up, but Mo B didn't need a declaration of his innocence. He'd known Jay since they were kids and he knew his boy would never do something so foul to a member of his own family.

As the two of them talked, Mo B caught Jay up to speed on everything that's been poppin' in the hood since he left. He told him all about the recent rash of murders that had been happening around the city, and how some new niggas from out of town been tryna takeover Omar's old territory.

"Who the fuck are these niggas," Jay questioned, "And where the fuck they from?"

"It's some nigga from Cali by the name of X. I don't know who he's working for, but I do know he's already recruited several members from the team. Lil Ray Ray from the eastside told me he's offering niggas double what Omar was paying if they joined his squad."

Jay couldn't fault Lil Ray Ray or any of the other workers for taking that deal. Niggas had to eat. But if his return to the game was going to work, Jay needed all the manpower he could get.

"Listen, I got a few more weeks of physical therapy to go before I make a full recovery. Once I do, I need everybody to be ready. I need you to call a team meeting for me so I can let everybody know what's up. Tell everybody to meet you at the old spot and then call me back at this number once everybody's there."

"Bet." Mo B agreed with no questions asked. He was more than ready to get shit poppin'. Although X had reached out to him too, Mo B politely declined his offer. His pockets were getting thinner by the day and he could've really used the money, but something about that nigga just didn't sit right with him. Having worked as one of Omar's top runners for more than six years, Mo B was trained to spot a shiesty nigga from a hundred miles away, and X definitely fit the bill.

After the two men wrapped up their conversation, Jay ended the call and tucked the cell phone underneath his mattress. He hoped that nigga X was ready, cause shit for him and his crew just got real.

CHAPTER SIXTEEN

Alaska spent the last week shadowing alongside Santee' and the other ladies as they went over every detail of the operation with her. She was assigned a crew of eight workers to assist her with transporting orders and collecting money. She was also given two bodyguards to help look out for her at all times. Santee' took her on a tour of the main warehouse and introduced her to the staff. He gave her the do's and dont's of the operation with the most important rule being to never show up there unannounced. Doing so was like a distress signal to the workers inside. The warehouse ran on a strict pickup and delivery schedule authorized only by Santee'. Any arrivals or departures deviating from that were automatically met with hostility.

Once Santee' was sure Alaska knew all she needed to know, he gave her the okay to start taking orders. Now she was sitting at the desk in the corner her bedroom contacting all of Omar's former customers one by one to let them know she was taking over. Just like Santee' told her too, Alaska quoted different prices for each person depending on their location. By her fifth call Alaska was feeling like a pro. She was getting so good that she was able to talk a young hustler from Flint, Michigan into paying her double what he normally would per brick. Even though he knew she was taxing him something serious, he was in a bind so he still placed an order for fifteen bricks. Just like that, Alaska racked in almost fifty thousand dollars from just that one transaction.

This shit is too fuckin' easy, she laughed to herself as she hung up the phone.

Alaska got up from the desk and headed to the kitchen to pour herself a glass of wine. She marveled at the fact that she had just been given entry into the dope game without ever having to slang a rock or hug a block. She was making moves normally reserved for those in the upper echelon of the game, and she wondered if Omar was proud. As she walked through the living room, she stopped to look at the pictures that decorated her mantel. She stared at images that represented a much happier time, and Alaska realized that she hadn't even spoken to Andraya since she saw her last week at the rehab facility. She had been so busy dealing with Santee' and the housewives, she hadn't even taken the time to call and make sure her girl was alright. While Alaska felt a little guilty for neglecting her friend, she couldn't overlook the fact that Andraya hadn't attempted to check in on her lately either. After all, Alaska was the one who lost her husband, not Draya. And honestly, she felt like she should be the one always being tended to and checked on.

Alaska realized she was the stronger of the two women, and that being the supportive friend was just her natural role, but sometimes it just became overwhelming to always have to hold someone else's hand in times of crisis. For just once, Alaska wished she could have the option of breaking down and completely falling apart when life didn't go her way. She knew that would never happen. Alaska was a boss now, and bosses only knew how to play the game with the hands they were dealt.

Retrieving a bottle of Moscato from the stainless steel refrigerator, Alaska went over to the cabinet and took out a wine glass. She filled the glass halfway and was about to take her first sip when she heard her cell phone ringing from the bedroom. Taking the wine glass and the bottle of wine with her, Alaska rushed back to her room to retrieve the phone.

"Hello," she answered almost out of breath.

"Hey, Alaska. It's Sophia."

"Oh, hey girl," Alaska replied. "What's up?"

"Nothing much, I was just headed out to get grab some lunch and I was calling to see if you wanted to join me."

"Sure, why not? Are the other ladies coming too?" Alaska asked.

"Naw, it'll just be me and you. The rest of the ladies have all went back home."

"Back home?" Alaska questioned.

"Yeah. The other ladies make up our west coast operations team but I'm the only one that's stationed here in Nevada. Kim and Daphne live out in L.A., and Ta'Kiyha lives in Texas."

"Oh, okay," Alaska replied.

She was cool with it just being the two of them. In fact, she actually preferred it that way. Even though the other chicks were cool, Alaska just seemed to vibe better with Sophia then she did with the rest of the girls. Maybe it was their shared racial background, both women being mixed with African-American and Colombian bloodlines. Or maybe they just subconsciously bonded over their grief of having just lost their husband's to the game. Sophia told Alaska that her man Anthony was killed recently in a robbery outside their home. Whatever the reason for their connection, Alaska was just glad to finally have somebody around that truly understood what she was going through.

The ladies agreed to meet up for lunch in about an hour, but they continued to chit chat for a few more minutes before hanging up. Since Alaska was already dressed for the day, she decided to call Santee' and put in her orders before heading out to meet Sophia. As she read off the list of her sales, Alaska calculated her profits to be around seventy thousand dollars for the week. *Not bad for just a few days of work,* she thought as she finished off her glass of wine.

"Good job," Santee' praised. He was very impressed with her numbers. "I can see you're going to be a very valuable asset to the team already."

It only took her a week to generate the same amount of revenue that most of the other girls were bring in per month, and this made Santee' a very happy man.

"Thank you," Alaska said taking a moment to bask in the compliment.

"I'll have one of my men deliver your payment sometime tomorrow after all the drops are made." Since Santee' had a crew who handled everything, all Alaska had to do was sit back and collect her money.

"Sounds good to me," she replied, wrapping up their conversation.

As long as everything continued to run this smoothly, Alaska would have the money she needed to handle her business in no time at all.

✝ ✝ ✝ ✝ ✝

"Right this way, ladies." The hostess smiled brightly as she led Alaska and Sophia to their table. They chose a quiet seafood restaurant located off the strip so they could relax and not have to worry about tourists. Most people assumed that residents of Las Vegas loved to be on the strip. But nothing could be further from the truth when it came to the majority of the city's long time natives. Having to sit in ridiculously long traffic jams, and dealing with enormously large crowds of people was not most of their ideas of a good time. Just as the ladies sat down in their chairs, Alaska's cell phone rung and the caller ID notified her that it was Jay.

"Sorry, I need to take this," she apologized to Sophia.

"It's all good girl. Go 'head and handle yo business."

"Thanks." Hey, what's up?" Alaska said cheerfully into the phone. She hadn't talked to her friends in a while and she was glad to see that one of them had finally called to check on her. But her excitement would be short lived.

"Have you talked to Draya?" Jay questioned without even so much as a hello.

"Damn, hello to you too nigga," Alaska replied kicking herself for actually thinking he was calling to see how she was doing, "And no I haven't talked to her today. Why?"

"Cause I've been blowing up her fuckin' phone all day and she's not answering. She was supposed to be here two hours ago to help me with my physical therapy but she never showed up."

"Well maybe she's at home and she accidentally fell asleep. Did you try calling the house phone?"

"I've called every phone number that woman has. She hasn't been up here in almost two days so I'm guessing she should be pretty well rested by now," Jay said sarcastically.

"Two days?" Alaska frowned. It was one thing for Draya not to call her in the last few days, but for her not to check in with Jay either sent up a red flag.

"Why didn't you call me before now?" Alaska asked.

"Because I thought it was nothing. We got into an argument the other night before she left and I figured her not coming back yesterday was her way of teaching me a lesson. But now she's taking this bullshit too fuckin' far by ignoring my calls and missing my treatment."

"Listen, I'll try calling her to see what's up. She's probably still pissed off and in need of some chill time. The last few weeks have been stressful on everybody. Once I talk to her I'll let you know she's okay. But I can't force her to call you though, so you'll have to work that out by yourself. Now I gotta go. I'll talk to you later."

Alaska dropped her iPhone down into her purse and sighed heavily.

"Playing Dr. Phil today, huh?' Sophia chuckled.

Alaska rolled her eyes as she nodded her head in agreement. "Yes girl, story of my fuckin' life," Alaska said as both of the women started laughing. The waiter came over and took their food and drink orders as Alaska tried to clear her mind of Draya and Jay's current drama.

"So how have you been getting alone since the shooting? Are you okay?" Sophia asked, sounding genuinely concerned.

"Umm… I've been okay. I have my moments you know? It's easy to stay busy and make it through the day. But when night falls and I find myself all alone, it gets a little bit harder. I just really miss having him around." Alaska's voice began to shake as tears welled up inside the corners of her eyes.

"I'm sorry," Sophia said as she reached over and touched Alaska's hand. "That was rude of me. Forgive me for even bringing it up."

"It's okay," Alaska said, dabbing the corner of her eyes with her napkin.

"Just know that if you ever need someone to talk to, I'm here."

"Thank you." Alaska smiled.

"So how's your first week on the job going," Sophia asked changing the subject as she squeezed juice from a lemon slice into her glass of water.

"It's going great." Alaska said, happy to be talking about something else. "I never knew stackin' paper could be so easy."

"I know right! Shit is crazy. I got more dough comin' in on the regular then I even know what to do with. I'mma start wiping my ass with that shit in a minute," Sophia joked as she put her hand in the air signaling for Alaska to give her some play.

"Girl you so crazy," Alaska said crackin' up.

"I mean, I'm just sayin'," Sophia shrugging her shoulders in an it is what it is kind of way. "So have you gotten your outfit for Santee's annual white party yet?" she asked.

"What white party?" Alaska questioned. "Nobody told me anything about it."

"Really? I can't believe Santee' haven't told you about it yet. Well consider this your official invitation honey, 'cause trust me when I say this is one party yo ass don't wanna miss. The one he threw last year was so live it took me damn near a week to recuperate!"

"Damn, it's like dat?"

"And then some. I attended a few of them with Anthony when he was alive, and every last one of them was off the chain. Even Jay-Z and Diddy showed up one year."

"Well count me in," Alaska said as their food finally arrived.

Right as the ladies began to dig into their meals, Alaska got a surprise when she looked up and seen Andraya strolling through the restaurant's entrance. After talking to Jay earlier, Alaska wondered what was really going on since Draya looked as if she didn't have a care in the world. She watched as her best friend checked in with the hostess and then disappeared into the ladies room.

"I'll be right back." Alaska told Sophia as she got up and left the table. As she made her way to the bathroom, Alaska had a feeling something was up but she couldn't put her finger on what it was. She walked in to the bathroom and did a quick check under the stalls to make sure Draya was the only one inside, and then she stood there and waited until for her to emerge from the stall.

"Bitch, what the hell yo sneaky ass been up to?" Alaska questioned as soon as the stall door swung open. Andraya was momentarily startled but she quickly regained her composure once she saw Alaska standing there.

"Alaska! Girl you scared the shit out of me," Andraya said putting her right hand over her heart. The two women embraced and Alaska could feel that something wasn't quite right.

"What are you doing here? You never come on this side of town." Andraya asked still a little flustered.

"I was going to ask you the same thing." Alaska said as they released each other. "I talked to Jay a few minutes ago and he told me you haven't been up to the facility in two days. What's going on?"

The smile on Draya's face instantly faded. She didn't want to have this conversation in a public bathroom, but she knew it was finally time she told her girl how she really felt. The idea of being broke *and* having a man who was permanently confined to a wheelchair for the rest of his life was just more than she could handle.

"I can't take this shit no more Alaska. I thought I was going to be able to hold him down through all of this, but I just can't do it." Draya avoided eye contact with Alaska as she walked over to the sink and began to wash her hands. Even though she couldn't help the way she felt, she still didn't want to see the disappointment in her best friend's eyes as she tried to explain her disloyalty.

"I love him to death, but I don't know if I love him enough to spend the rest of our lives pushing him around in that fuckin' chair. If he ends up confine to that thing the quality of our lives will be drastically different. I'll be broke, sexless and miserable, and that ain't what the hell I signed up for."

As Draya dried her hands with a paper towel, Alaska looked at her friend very closely. She could see the stress and strain behind Draya's eyes and she instantly felt guilty for not being there for her girl. It was obvious she was breaking down and if Alaska been around more, she would have noticed the signs.

"Listen, I think that's just the stress talking. I know it's hard and dealing with all of this is overwhelming, but you can do this." Alaska placed her hand on Draya's shoulder. "Besides, you can't just walk out on him now Draya. You gotta put your big girl panties on and boss the fuck up. That is your husband laid up in that hospital, not some random ass nigga you just met last week."

"I know, I know. But I'm just not built like you, Alaska. I don't know how to maintain like this." Andraya started to cry.

As Alaska grabbed her some tissue from the nearby stall, there was a faint knock on the bathroom's door.

"Draya, you alright in there?" A deep male voice questioned from the other side.

"Who the hell is that?" Alaska whispered with a puzzled look on her face.

"Shit. Xavier. I almost forgot he was out there."

"Xavier?" Alaska said in amazement. "Bitch, you can't be serious."

If Alaska wasn't sure her friend was falling apart before, she was definitely sure of it now.

"Listen, I know how bad this looks but please don't judge me right now, okay. We're only having lunch." Andraya cleared her throat and called out to her date, "Yeah, I'm fine. I'll be out in a minute."

Alaska realized that Draya was a grown woman and that there was no way she could control her actions. But she definitely felt like she needed to talk some sense into her best friend because it was clear she was losing her mind.

"Okay," Alaska quickly conceded. She knew Draya was fragile so the last thing she wanted to do was start a fight with her. "Why don't you just have Xavier drop you off at my house when y'all finish eating then? I got a couple bottles of wine and a quarter bag of kush that I copped from Money Mike last week. We can sit back, talk shit and get fucked up just like old times. Cool?"

"Yeah, that sounds cool," Andraya smiled. "I'll see you in a few hours." She dried her eyes and fixed her make-up before the two of them headed for the door. Just Alaska reached for the handle, Sophia came rushing in.

"Damn girl, I thought you fell in or something," she joked, "You alright?"

Andraya gave Alaska a *who the fuck is this bitch face*, but she didn't bother to stick around for an introduction. Instead she used the distraction to avoid the clash she knew was coming once Alaska and Xavier saw one another. Exiting the bathroom in a hurry, Draya told Alaska that she would see her later on at the house.

But as Alaska stood there trying to figure out what the hell just happened, her instincts told her that she probably wouldn't be seeing Draya again anytime soon.

CHAPTER SEVENTEEN

Jay flipped through the same ten channels on the hospital's TV for what seemed like the millionth time. He still hadn't heard back from Draya and he was starting to think that something maybe wrong. He called her cell phone more than a hundred times since yesterday morning and every single one of his calls went unanswered. Jay had called and texted her so much that now his calls were going straight to voicemail.

"ARGGG," Jay yelled out in frustration. He was so pissed off that he pulled the phone from the plug and flung it across the room. Just as it was about to crash into the wall, Nurse Fatty came walking through the door.

"What the fuck," she said, ducking for cover. When the phone finally made contact with the wall, the handset slammed into a framed painting shattering it into a thousand pieces.

"Umm ... I can see this isn't a good time for you. I'll just come back later." Sharonda said as she quickly began to back out of the room.

"Naw, its cool, ma. You can come in."

"You sure?" she asked examining the pile of broken glass on the floor. Jay nodded and waved her inside.

"Are you alright?"

"Yeah, I'm cool. Just got some shit on my mind that's all. What's up with you though?"

"Not too much," she said walking over to his bed. "I got some more goods from my baby daddy and I thought I would stop by and bring you some." Nurse Fatty pulled a Ziploc bag full of weed from her purse and handed it to Jay.

"That's what's up. Thanks ma." Jay opened the bag and put it to his nose. "Damn, that's some good shit. Your baby daddy got it like that, huh?"

Sharonda shrugged her shoulders.

"I guess so." She replied, rolling her eyes. "I don't really fuck with him like that, but every now and then he'll hit me off with some greens in an effort to stay in my good graces. It's really the only thing he's good for." Sharonda placed her purse on the nightstand and took a seat in the chair next to Jay's bed. "But enough about his bum ass, I came here to see you?"

"Word," Jay grinned seductively. "Well here I am."

He was still pissed off at Draya and he knew Nurse Fatty was exactly what he needed to get his mind off things. Rubbing his growing hard on, Jay instructed her to lock the door. Sharonda did as she was told, without speaking she stripped down to her underwear and mounted him like a horse. Jay admired her body as he ran his hands over her smooth, cocoa brown skin. He removed one of her breast from the red satin bra she was wearing and ran his tongue across her nipple. The sensation sent a chill up her spine and she moaned out in pleasure.

"I wanna eat that pussy," Jay whispered in her ear. "Turn around and let me see it."

Sharonda reversed her position, putting her ass directly in Jay's face. Since they began messing around a few weeks ago, Jay had never eaten her pussy and she couldn't wait to test out his skills. Spreading her ass cheeks, Jay got a bird's eye view of the juiciest pair of pussy lips he'd ever seen in his life. The inside of her flower was the perfect shade of pink and outside was freshly shaven, making his dick grow even harder. Grabbing her hips, he pulled her pussy closer to his face and slowly ran the tip of his tongue across her clit.

"Mmm ... that feels so good, baby." Sharonda cooed, while winding her hips in a circular motion. Her face was buried in his crotch so she reached into his pants and pulled his dick out, placing it into her mouth. Intertwined in the sixty-nine position and feeling like they both had something to prove, each of them tried their best to outdo the other. A chorus of moans and slurps were the only sounds heard throughout the room as the two of them got it in. They were so focused, that neither of them heard the knocking on Jay's door.

"Turn around," Jay suddenly commanded. He didn't want her to know that she was currently winning their little battle for best head giver, so he had to make her stop. If he allowed her to keep going he knew he would only end up embarrassing himself by cuming too soon. However, when she slid her warm, juicy pussy over his rock hard dick, Jay realized that it didn't matter if she was sucking or fucking him. Either way, the eruption building inside his nuts was going to be extremely hard to keep at bay.

Riding Jay like a stallion, Nurse Fatty cupped both of her breasts and bounced up and down on his dick, tightening her pussy muscles with each stroke. Jay palmed her ass and guided his manhood deeper into her flower.

"That pussy feel good to you, daddy?" Sharonda cooed.

Jay was just about to tell her how much when he heard a knock at the door.

KNOCK! KNOCK! KNOCK!

"Security!" yelled the old white man on the other side of the door. "You okay in there?" Before Jay could respond, the lock turn over and the door swung open.

"Oh my," the security guard grasped, more in response to Sharonda's naked body then to the sexual acts they were committing. "I .... I'm sorry. Please forgive me."

The old man tried to back out of the room and close the door, but it was too late. Marybeth, one of the facility administrators, came strolling down the hall.

"Oh Charlie, I see you're already on it," Marybeth said walking towards him. "Mrs. Montgomery here just informed me she couldn't gain access to her husband's room because the door was locked. Is everything okay?"

Hearing Draya's name caused Jay's heart to drop. His reflexes took over and caused him to push Nurse Fatty from his lap. Her naked body fell to the cold hard floor just as Andraya emerged in the doorway.

"What the fuck!" Andraya screamed, instantly enraged. She pushed pass Marybeth and the security guard, fully entering the room. Without warning, Draya picked up a glass vase filled with flowers and lunged it at Sharonda, missing her head by only a few inches. Just as she was about to go into beat a bitch mode, another security guard enter the room and snatched her up.

"Get the fuck off of me," Draya yelled as she tried to loosen his grip. She looked like a complete fool with her arms and legs swinging wildly in front of her as the guard held her tightly by the waist. When she realized he wasn't letting go she decided to give up the fight. Breathlessly, she turned to Jay.

"Nigga, you ain't shit."

"Baby, I'm so sorry." Jay said, finally managing to speak. "I had a weak moment and I fucked up."

"That's bullshit. And who the fuck is this bitch anyway?" Draya spat as she pointed to Sharonda.

"That," Marybeth stepped in, "is a nurse who unfortunately just lost her job." She picked up Sharonda's clothes from the floor and handed them to her. "Get dressed. I want to see you in my office immediately."

"No need," Sharonda replied. She slipped on her clothes and handed Marybeth her badge. "I'll clean out my locker and be outta her in five minutes."

Sharonda knew there would be consequence to her actions if she ever got caught so there was no point in crying wolf now. Embarrassed but with her head still held high, she grabbed her purse from the nightstand and proceeded to exit the room. As she walked past Draya, the two of them locked eyes.

"You betta never let me catch you in the streets, bitch. 'Cause I swear to God I'mma try and knock yo' fucking head off your shoulders."

Sharonda ignored Draya's threat and continued to make her way out of the room. There was a whole lot she wanted to say in response, but she didn't want to fuck her day up any further by getting an unnecessary assault charge. Jay felt guilty as he lay there helplessly watching the scene unfold. He never meant for Sharonda to lose her job, and he definitely never meant for Draya to find out about them.

"Baby," Jay called out to her in a voice that was barely above a whisper, "please come over here so I can talk to you."

"Fuck you! And don't call me baby." Andraya was hot and there was nothing Jay could do to pacify her in this moment. "Here I am running around stressed out and praying that everything turns out okay, meanwhile you're sticking your dick in anything that moves. Well you know what, that bitch can have yo dirty dick ass 'cause I'm done." Andraya directed her attention back to Marybeth, "Unless he's dead or dying, don't call my fucking phone. As of this very moment, I no longer give a fuck!"

Before Jay could even get the words out of his mouth to beg her to stay, Andraya was storming down the hallway headed back to her car.

"FUCK!" Jay yelled unable to believe his spot had just been blown. Shit for him couldn't get any worse than it was right now and Jay was becoming seriously vexed because of it. When he noticed Marybeth was still standing in his room, he decided to take some of his anger out on her.

"What the fuck you still standing there for?"

"Mr. Montgomery, I would appreciate if you would re-frain from speaking to me that way. I just wanted to let you know that we don't condone the type of behavior you and Ms. Fatty exhibited today in our facility. As long as you're a patient here nothing like that can ever happen again, other-wise, I will be forced to discontinue your care and discharge you from this center."

"Listen, as long as the balance on my account says ze-ro, I will continue to be a patient at this ratchet ass facility for as long as I please. Now leave me the fuck alone and get the hell outta my room." Jay knew he was wrong for being so rude, but right now he didn't care. He felt like she was judg-ing him as she stood there with a smirk on her face and he didn't like that feeling.

"Mr. Montgomery, I'm sorry to inform you but the bal-ance on your account is currently eight thousand, six hundred fifty two dollars, and nineteen cents." Marybeth grabbed his chart from the wall and flipped through it. "It looks like a payment hasn't been made to your account in over a month."

Jay was speechless. Andraya had access to every dime of the two hundred thousand dollars he had saved up, and she assured him just last week that she had been taking care of all the bills.

"So like I was saying," Marybeth continued, "either correct your behavior, or find yourself another rehabilitation center."

And with that, she walked out of the room leaving Jay alone to stew in his own juices.

CHAPTER EIGHTEEN

Andraya

The moment Draya was out of the facility and back inside of her car she began to laugh hysterically. The reason she had come there in the first place was to finally break the news to Jay about how she had been feeling. She was planning to tell him she needed a break, and that she thought they should separate for a little while. She was worried that abandoning him when he needed her most would make her look shady, but she was willing to do whatever she had to do. However, Draya got the shock of her life when she entered Jay's room, and she couldn't believe her luck when she saw what was going down. As twisted as it sounds, and even though everyone there thought she was upset, Draya was actually ecstatic that she now had a valid reason to walk away from her marriage.

Dropping the top on her cherry red Mustang, Draya merged onto the freeway headed towards her house. She was hoping Xavier was still there sleeping in her bed just as he was when she left. After the way he put his dick game down when they left the bar the other night, Draya was convinced her decision to separate from Jay was for the best. Not because she thought Xavier was going to be the answer to all her prayers, but instead because she welcomed the freedom to be able to fuck him, or anybody else for that matter, whenever she chose.

Rihanna's new song "Birthday Cake" was playing on the radio and Draya sang along. Just as she was about to turn up the volume, she heard her cell phone ringing and she grabbed it out of her purse.

"Hello"

"Hey, it's Xavier. I woke up looking for you. Where'd you go?"

Draya smiled into the phone, "I had to make a run, but I'm on my way back now. I should be then in less than ten minutes."

"Well hurry back. I got some business to take care so I'll have to go soon. But I definitely need another shot of that ass before I do."

Just hearing his voice made Draya's panties wet and she couldn't wait to get back home. She pressed the bottom of her Louboutin's against the gas pedal and accelerated the car's speed to 90. In no time, she was pulling into the driveway of the home she once happily shared with Jay. As she parked her car and hopped out, Draya noticed one of her neighbors staring at her from across the street.

"Hey, Mrs. Bradley," Draya said waving at the old woman. "How are you today?"

"Oh, I'm fine honey, thanks for asking. Say, I thought I saw a young fella come outside this morning and get your newspaper. Is your husband finally back home?"

Andraya chuckled. When Mrs. Bradley asked her a few weeks ago why Jay hadn't been around, Draya lied and told her that he was out of town on business. Being the old school woman that she was, Mrs. Bradley told Draya that she thought it was a bad sign for a man to be gone from his wife for so long. She would say absence doesn't make the heart grow fonder; it just leaves room for somebody else to come in and take your place.

In a way, Draya realized Mrs. Bradley was right. Jay being in the nursing home for the last few months made her realize that being married to him, especially now that he was cripple and broke, was no longer what she wanted.

HEAVY

"No Mrs. Bradley he's still away. That must have been my cousin you saw this morning. He's here visiting me from out of town."

Mrs. Bradley raised her eyebrow, "Oh, I see. Well you two kids enjoy your day. I have to take Mr. Bradley to the doctor soon so I better run. See you later, honey."

"Okay, Mrs. Bradley. I'll see you later."

Andraya smiled and shook her head as she walked up the pathway to her front door. That lady was nosey as shit, but Andraya loved her to death. She hadn't spoken to her own mother in over ten years and in a way, Mrs. Bradley helped to fill that void.

Andraya walked into the house and tossed her bag on the sofa before heading upstairs to her bedroom. Anxious to get some more of Xavier's good loving, she began taking her clothes off along the way. By the time she made it to the door, the only thing she was wearing was a La Perla underwear set and her favorite pair of red bottoms.

"Damn," Xavier said when he finally looked up and saw her standing in the doorway. He was sitting on the edge of the bed with his shirt off, going through his phone. "Dat's how you greet a nigga? Straight like that?"

"Straight like that," Draya replied as she walked over and sat on his lap. "I just got some great news and I couldn't wait to come home and celebrate by bouncing on your dick."

"Is that right?" He smirked. Andraya nodded her head yes, and then she began to leave a trail of wet kisses down the side of his neck. "Well, I hate to do this, but can you hold that thought for a minute 'cause I gotta make a quick run?"

"What … Why?" Andraya's smile faded and she poked her lips out like a little girl.

"I gotta go handle some business. I've been locked up in this room with you for the last few days, and the streets are moving without me. I'm missing money ma, and I just can't have that. Give me like two hours tops and I promise I'll be right back here to dig your back out."

Xavier grabbed the back of her head and kissed her so passionately, she had no choice but to give in. With her legs still wrapped around his waist, Xavier stood up, turned around and laid Draya gently onto the bed. "Now, stay exactly like that and I'll be back before you know it."

Draya propped herself up on her elbows and smiled. She watched him put on the rest of his clothes before grabbing her robe and walked him to the front door. As they walked through the living room, she could see him glancing at some of the pictures she had on display.

"You still miss him don't you?" Xavier asked once they got to the door.

"Who?"

"Your husband," he said pointing to a picture mounted above her fireplace. "I heard he was killed a few months back."

Andraya chuckled. "That's just what everybody thinks. He took a few shots during a robbery, but he's still alive and recuperating at a private facility. And as far as him being my husband, that won't be the case for too much longer."

A sudden grin washed over Xavier's face.

"What's so funny?" Draya asked.

"Nothing, I was just smiling at how beautiful you are." Xavier kissed her on the cheek and headed out the door. Andraya watched until his Tahoe disappeared from view, and then she shut the door.

Since she had some time to kill before Xavier returned, Draya decided to get dressed and head over to Alaska's. She knew her girl was pissed that she stood her up, and she wanted to apologize. She also needed to tell her about the situation that jumped off at the nursing home today. Draya couldn't wait to see the look on Alaska's face when she told her. To Alaska, Jay was practically family and whenever they had a disagreement, Draya always felt like she took his side.

Heading back to her bedroom, Draya picked up the clothes she had thrown onto the floor earlier. As soon as she slipped the Gucci maxi dress over her head, she heard her cell phone ringing and she rushed to retrieve it from her purse but she was too late. Glancing down at the screen, Draya saw she had sixty-five missed calls and messages, all from Jay.

Nigga please, Draya thought as she tossed the phone back into her purse without even checking her messages. There wasn't anything Jay could say to her at this point that would make her stay. Her mind was already made up and as far as she was concerned, their relationship was a wrap. First thing tomorrow morning, Draya planned to pay a realtor a visit so she could find herself a new place to stay. Something in the far corner of her mind was telling her she should wait, but Draya ignored the notion.

Grabbing her purse off the couch, Draya took out her keys and headed for the door. Just as she turned the knob, someone began beating on the door from the other side.

"Who is it?" Draya called out.

When she didn't get a response, Draya reluctantly swung open the door and got the got the surprise of her life when she saw who was standing there.

"Hey Draya. Did you miss me?"

CHAPTER NINETEEN

Alaska

Alaska plugged her iPod into the portable stereo speakers, and selected a track from Melanie Fiona's new CD, *The MF Life,* before pressing play. As Melanie's sultry voice flowed through the speakers, Alaska removed her clothes and turned on the shower. It had been almost two whole days since she saw Draya at the restaurant, just as she suspected, she still hadn't heard from her. Alaska was having mixed feelings about the things Draya told her. While she had no idea what it was like to be in her girl's shoes, she still was unable to comprehend how Draya could just abandon Jay like that. After everything the two of them had been through together, after all the times Jay had been there for her, Alaska felt like Draya needed to suck it up and try harder to make things work.

Making sure the water wasn't too hot; Alaska pulled back the shower curtain and stepped inside. Just as water began to dance all over her body, she heard her doorbell ring. "Got dammit!" Alaska said as she reached for her robe. She got out of the shower and wrapped the soft terry cloth fabric around her body without tying it up. Leaving a trial of water puddles behind her, Alaska made her way from the bathroom to the front door.

Since she wasn't expecting anybody, she figured it was probably Andraya and she didn't bother looking through the peephole before she swung the door open, ready to go off.

HEAVY

"Bitc …" Alaska stopped her tirade mid-sentence when she realized it was Santee' standing on the other side of the door and not Draya.

"Oh shit. Umm... Hey Santee'," she said as she fumbled around trying to close up her robe, "My bad, I thought you were my home girl."

"No, forgive me. I should have called first." Santee' apologized but he didn't even pretend to look away from Alaska's naked body. He had been attracted to her since the first day they met and he welcomed any opportunity he could to get a closer look at her beauty.

"It's okay. Come on in," Alaska said as she tried to pull herself together. She was still soaking wet and water was dripping from everywhere so she told Santee' to make himself comfortable while she went to go change.

When Alaska made it to her room she couldn't help but smile at the way Santee' was checking her out. After she dried herself off, she didn't even bother putting on any underwear as she slipped on a pair of pink sweats and a black tank top. Alaska grabbed a brush off her dresser and quickly whipped her hair up into a ponytail. Her skin was becoming dry from the quick dip in the shower, so Alaska grabbed the jar of cherry-almond scented Shea butter that she ordered from Carol's Daughter, and she rubbed it on the parts of her body that were exposed. After making sure she looked okay, Alaska lightly sprayed on a little bit of her favorite Prada perfume.

Alaska could feel butterflies inside her stomach as she made her way back to the living room. Although she was reluctant to admit it to herself, she did feel some kind of way whenever Santee' was around. As she admired his muscular six-foot tall frame and his smooth butter-pecan complexion, a waterfall began to form between her thighs and Alaska had to try hard to retain her composure.

"Sorry to keep you waiting," she said as she walked back into the room. "Can I get you a drink or something?"

"No I'm fine," Santee' said as he got up from the couch and handed Alaska an envelope. "I just came by to bring your money."

"What happened to Tommy?" Alaska asked, referring to her normal delivery guy.

"He was sick so I decided to just bring it myself."

"Oh," Alaska said, placing the envelope on the coffee table, "Well thank you, I appreciate it. You sure I can't get you anything to drink? I practically have a full bar over here."

"Well in that case," Santee' smiled and took his seat back on the couch. "Let me get a double shot of **Patrón**."

"Coming right up."

Andraya walked over to the wet bar and grabbed the bottle of **Patrón, two shot glasses and several slices of limes.** Before returning to the living room, she hit the power button on the stereo filling the room with Beyonce's sultry voice. After preparing their drinks, she took two slices of lime and stuck a tiny umbrella through each one before placing them in the glasses.

"Here you go," she smiled as she handed Santee' his glass.

"Thank you, beautiful."

Alaska sat down next to him, all of a sudden she felt nervous. The butterflies inside her stomach returned, and she could feel her palms begin to sweat.

"Let's toast," Santee said, raising his glass in the air and motioning for Alaska to do the same. "To success, longevity and prosperity; may we forever be blessed with all three."

"Ditto," Alaska said as their glasses clinked together. Hoping to calm her nerves, she quickly tossed the liquor to the back of her throat and forced it down before immediately pouring herself another one.

"I make you nervous don't I?"

"What makes you say that?" Alaska replied, somewhat caught off guard.

"Because whenever you're around me you start drinking like a fish. So I figure either you must be nervous, or you're just a lush."

Alaska giggled. "I'm definitely not a lush. I just like to have a drink or two sometimes to take the edge off."

"That's cool. But it still doesn't answer my question though."

"To be honest," Alaska replied, "at times you do make me a little nervous. But I guess that's just because I haven't been this close to another man since Omar died."

"Well don't worry, although I'm extremely attracted to you, I promise I won't try to take advantage of you."

"But what if I wanted you to?" Alaska asked shyly. The liquor was working its way through her bloodstream She couldn't believe those words had just slipped from her mouth.

"Then I would be forced to oblige your request." Santee' said, as he gently placed his hand on her cheek. "Is that what you want?"

Alaska didn't answer. Instead she kissed him softly on the lips. Santee' pulled her body in closer to his, and wrapped his arms around her waist. The smell of her perfume was intoxicating and he inhaled it deeply as he left kisses along her collarbone. Santee's hands began to explore her body, and a soft moan escaped from Alaska's lips as she threw her head back in ecstasy. Although it had only been a few months, it felt like years had passed since the last time she enjoyed a feeling this good.

Alaska grabbed Santee's hand and she began leading him to her bedroom. Santee' couldn't help but notice her voluptuous ass which was bulging from the back of her sweatpants as they walked down the hallway. He also noticed a small tattoo of Omar's name with the dates representing his birth and death on the nape of her neck. Alaska represented for her late husband even in his death, and that turned Santee' on. Loyalty was the number one thing he looked for in a woman, Alaska definitely had it.

When Alaska opened the door to her bedroom, "Unthinkable" by Alicia Keys was playing from the speakers she had set up in the bathroom. Alaska listened to Alicia sing about the exact same thing she was feeling as she walked over to her bed and laid down. She watched as Santee' began to remove his clothes, and her eyes roamed all over his toned body. Santee' reminded her of the Spanish pop singer Enrique Iglesias, but the only difference was that Santee' was slightly older and he possessed a lot more swag. With his pants now off, Alaska got a glimpse of what Santee' was working with and she smiled in satisfaction. Her pussy was already jumping and she couldn't wait to feel him inside of her.

Alaska pulled back the covers, inviting Santee' into her bed. But when she looked down at the sheets, the picture of Omar that she slept with every night was staring back at her. Tears instantly filled her eyes as the realization of what she was doing entered her mind.

"What's wrong?" Santee' asked looking down to see what caused the change in her demeanor. He saw the picture and without saying a word, he picked it up and placed it back on her nightstand. Santee' then climbed into the bed with Alaska and wrapped his arms around her, holding her in complete silence as warm tears continued to roll down her cheeks.

"I'm sorry," she whispered with her face buried in his chest.

"Shhh … its okay mi amor, you don't owe me any apologies," Santee' whispered while stroking her hair. "I respect the bond you had with Omar and I completely understand if you're not ready. You're an amazing woman Alaska Drake, and I would wait until the end of time to have the chance to be with you."

Santee's words made Alaska feel special, but her attraction to him still made her feel as if she was betraying Omar. Even though she knew he would want her to be happy, she felt like she was breaking some kind of code by hooking up with a man he once considered a friend. As a thousand different thoughts ran through her mind, Alaska laid there in Santee's arms as she cried herself into a deep sleep.

The next morning when Alaska woke up, she could still smell the scent of Santee's cologne lingering in her bed even though he was no longer there. She pulled the covers over her head and saw that it was damn near one o'clock in the afternoon. She tried to recall the moment Santee' had actually left, but she was sleeping like a baby and hadn't heard a thing. As she sat up in her bed, she looked over Omar's picture and let out a deep breath. She knew at some point she was going to have to move on, and something inside was telling her that Santee' might be the one to help her do it.

She picked up the picture frame and placed her lips to the glass one last time before she tucked it away in the top drawer of the nightstand. Alaska decided after she handled her unfinished business with Omar's killer, she would finally close this chapter in her life and move on. She still loved Omar with all her heart but she didn't want to be lonely forever.

Alaska climbed out of the bed and headed to the bathroom to finish taking the shower she never got around to taking last night. After she got dressed and did her hair, Alaska checked the messages on her cell phone to see if she had any new sales. *"Another day, another dollar,"* Alaska said as she thumbed through all of her text messages. The money she was making was so easy, she contemplated hipping Draya to the game so that her girl could make some extra money too.

But then Alaska remembered how incapable her home girl was at bossing up and handling business so she knew it probably wouldn't work.

Right as she dismissed the notion, Alaska's cell phone began to ring and Draya's face appeared on the screen.

"So you stood me up for Xavier's bitch ass, huh?" Alaska wasted no time going in on her girl as soon as she answered the phone.

"My bad, but I promise it wasn't even like that," Draya said apologizing. "Since I saw you that night, you wouldn't believe all the shit that's gone down."

"Try me," Alaska said, eager to hear her explanation.

"It's a long story, but break out the kush and a bottle of wine because I'll be in your driveway in five minutes."

Alaska shook her head as she hung up the phone and she went to her bedroom to retrieve her stash. She grabbed the Swisser Sweets box where she keep all of her smoking supplies from underneath her bed and took it into the living room. By the time she went to the kitchen to get a bottle of wine and some glasses, Draya was already ringing her doorbell. Even though she could see her car from the living room window, Alaska still looked through the peephole this time before she opened the door.

"Hey," Draya sang as she walked through the door and gave Alaska a hug.

"What's up girl, you looking cute today," Alaska said as she complimented Draya's attire.

The two friends went into the living room and took a seat on Alaska's chocolate brown, Italian leather couch. As they began to chat and catch up, Alaska took out one of the cigarillos and started to roll up. She split open the cigar and dumped out the tobacco inside, replacing it with a small amount of weed. After she perfectly rerolled the cigarillo back into its original shape, she took a lighter out of her purse and lit the tip. She took a few pulls from the blunt then passed it over to Draya as they sat there in silence allowing the THC to flow through their bloodstreams. Draya hit the blunt a little too hard and began to cough from the burning smoke inside her lungs.

"Whoa, you betta be easy bitch," Alaska said laughing. "That ain't like that oregano type shit we used to smoke back in the day. This shit right here will have yo' ass fucked up." Alaska grabbed the blunt back from Draya and took a puff.

Once the ladies developed a nice buzz, Andraya began telling her story. Starting from the night she ran into Xavier at the bar. Draya ran down everything that happened since then, sparing no details. By the time she got to the part about the surprise visitor who showed up on her doorstep, Alaska mouth was hanging wide open.

"So who was it?" she asked, wondering if Draya's story could get any crazier.

"Carmen."

"As in your sister, Carmen?" Alaska frowned.

"Yup, the one and only. I haven't seen or heard from her ass in six years and she just shows up on my doorstep out of the blue, asking for a favor."

"What kind of favor?"

"She said my mother is sick and needs a kidney transplant. She wanted me to come down to the hospital and get tested to see if I may be a match."

"Wow. What did you tell her?" Alaska asked, taking another pull from the blunt.

"I told her ass to kick rocks. What you think I told her? Her and my mother turned their backs on me at a time when I could barely fend for myself. For them to even think I would be willing to lift a finger to help them out is beyond my comprehension."

"But that's your mother," Alaska said stunned at Draya's response. She knew the two of them had an estranged relationship but she always assumed that Draya still had love for her mother.

"That didn't mean shit to her when she kicked me out of her house pregnant and broke," Draya spat. "I called her every day for weeks begging her to let me come home and all she did was turn her back on me. Even when the fight with Carmen caused me to have a miscarriage, she still wouldn't let me come back. As far as I'm concerned, she may as well be dead already because I could care less."

Alaska could see the tears welling up in the corners of Draya's eyes and she reached out to give her friend a hug. Although she played tough, Alaska knew deep down Draya really did care. But she also knew that her friend was very bull headed so to try and get her to change her mind at this point would be damn near impossible. Hoping to lighten the mood, she decided to change the subject and finally tell Draya about Santee and the other housewives. Draya's expression quickly changed from sadness to excitement when Alaska told her how much money she had been making.

"Damn bitch, you been holding out on me," Draya said shocked that Alaska hadn't told her about this sooner. "You gotta hook me up so I can get down too. With all I got going on, I could really use some dough like that right about now."

"I'll see what I can do," Alaska replied. "But entrance into the Cocaine Housewives club is by invitation only. Santee' hand picks the members and I'm not sure if I can just convince him to let you in. I might be able to get you a little side work though, but you gotta make sure you keep it on the low. You can't even tell Jay," Alaska warned.

"I got you girl. Just get me in and I promise I won't let you down." Draya replied.

Alaska took the last hit of the blunt and prayed she didn't end up regretting her offer.

CHAPTER TWENTY

Xavier strolled through the lobby of the newly built Aria Resort and Casino, looking like money. He was rocking a crispy pair of Louis Vuitton jeans with a matching brown Louis Vuitton t-shirt which sported the famous "LV" logo prominently on the front. His freshly touched up dreads hung just past his shoulders and the three karat diamond studs he wore in each ear were shinning underneath the lobby's fluorescent lights. Xavier could have used the private entrance designated for guest of the penthouse suites, but he preferred to be seen. Hotel lobby's in Vegas were always filled with beautiful women looking to have fun, and Xavier was always ready to accommodate them. As he made his way to the penthouse elevators, he saw one of his recent conquests sitting at the bar with her husband. As they caught eye contact, she winked to let him know that she was ready for round two whenever he was. When her husband turned his back, she put two fingers up to her ear, signaling for Xavier to call her. Feeling like the man, Xavier stepped onto the elevator and swiped his card.

"Hello, Mr. Cruz. Welcome back to the Aria." The elevator's automated computer system greeted him. *"The estimated time of arrive to your suite is less than fifteen seconds. Enjoy the ride and have a great evening."*

The doors to the elevator closed and as it began to ascend, Xavier pulled out his phone to check his text messages. He was tired as shit from all the ripping, running and fucking he'd been doing over the last few days. He was glad to finally be back home. Even if the home was currently a tricked out hotel suite. As the elevator made it to his floor, a text message came through and vibrated his phone.

My pussy is soaking wet & I'm feining for some more of that dick. Can I come up? Xavier shook his head. The message was from the jump off he'd just seen at the bar on his way up. He texted her back,

Where's ur husband?

Who gives a fuck?

"Clearly not you," Xavier laughed to himself as he opened the door to his suite. He was just about to tell her to come up when he heard the sound of the TV playing in the next room, and he realized somebody was there.

"Who dat," he called out as he instinctively pulled the .50 cal heater from the waistline of his jeans. When he didn't get an answer, Xavier removed the gun's safety and slowly proceeded to the room. "I said, who the fuck is that," he repeated. When he rounded the corner, he was able to see the back of a blue New Era fitted cap peeking over the top of the oversized pillows that lined the couch. He had his gun aimed and ready to shoot.

"Nigga put that muthafuckin gun down 'fore I take that bitch from you and shoot you in the kneecap wit it."

When he heard his boss's voice, Xavier put the gun back in his waistband and walked around to the other side of the couch. "Fuck you nigga," he joked, "And what the hell you doing up in my spot anyway?"

"Your spot? Nigga if I ain't mistaken, the ten thou a night it cost for you to stay in this muthafucka is coming out of *my* pockets. So If I were you, I would be a little more grateful." Big Hank said matter-of-factly.

Xavier didn't respond cause he hated the fact that he was currently depending upon his boss to live. Five years ago, shit was the other way around and Xavier was at the top of his game while Big Hank was still struggling to come up.

But after spending the last two years in jail on drug charge, Xavier went back home to California only to find a whole new crew of niggas running the streets he once claimed. Everybody in his crew, from corner boys to lieutenants all jumped ship and signed on with the other team. By the time Xavier made it home, the drug empire he spent years building and cultivating, had completely crumbled. The only thing he had left to show for his time in the game was a measly twenty thousand dollars in cash.

"But anyway," Big Hank continued, "I was in the neighborhood and I figured I would stop by and check on the progress of our little project."

A smile spread across Xavier's face. "It's going very well. I just found out that our boy Jay is still alive, and currently living at a highly secured nursing facility outside of the city. The spot is normally reserved for celebrities and politicians and it's so fuckin' private, it doesn't even have a name or a physical address. The only way to find it is by locating its' coordinates on a map, and I got my girl Yvette working on getting that information right now."

Yvette was Xavier's go to girl for pretty much everything. When Andraya confirmed that Jay was alive and in a nursing home, he gave that information to Yvette and with it she was able to get all the information he'd just given to Big Hank.

"Cool," Big Hank said as he stood up and headed to the door. "Hit me up when you get it."

Xavier nodded and once Hank was gone, he sat down on the couch and rolled up a blunt. Just as he was about to light the tip, his phone vibrated again with another text message.

Hey bae. What time u coming through?

This time, the message was from Andraya and Xavier smiled. Despite his actions, past and present, he truly did care for her. She was beautiful, intelligent, funny, and her sex game was fantastic. If the circumstances were different he probably would have made her his wife. But his connection to her husband's impending murder pretty much ensured that'll never happen.

When Xavier got out of jail three months ago, the only thing he had was the clothes on his back and the little bit of cash he had left behind with his mother. Within days of being back in the hood, Xavier realized the game had moved on without him and the only way for him to get back on top was to start from the bottom. He took a job working as a corner boy for an up and coming young hustler named Stevie. He would have been making a little less than a thousand dollars a week, but he quit after the first day. Xavier couldn't deal with a nigga as young and green as Stevie telling him what to do. It just didn't feel right.

Not long after that, Xavier ran into Big Hank at a strip club. As the two of them sat at the bar shooting the shit, Hank mentioned on a whim that he needed somebody to help him do a job. When Hank told him that the job paid fifty stacks, Xavier instantly accepted the work with questions asked. Hank then told him the back story of how the first shooting went wrong, leaving Jay alive. The next day after he'd learned the identity of his target, Xavier did his research and found that Jay was married to one of his old flings, Andraya. Needing the money now more than ever, Xavier was forced to walk back into Andraya's life only to leave her heartbroken for the second time around.

He knew she would probably never find out about his involvement, but he didn't think his conscience wouldn't allow him to stick around and watch her suffer once his job was complete. So for now, all he wanted to do was enjoy the little time they had left. He picked up his phone and replied to her text.

I'm on my way. Get that pussy wet for daddy!

Putting out the blunt, Xavier jumped in the shower and changed his clothes before he headed out to see Draya. The moment he stepped off the elevator and back into the lobby,

the jump off from earlier appeared by his side and Xavier
instantly wished he'd used the private elevator.

"There you are, sexy," she said looping her arm
through his, "I've been waiting for you to hit me back. Are
you ready for me to come up now?"

Xavier frowned. *Damn, this bitch is a fuckin' stalker,*
He thought as he removed her arm from his.

"Listen, I had a great time wit 'chu the other night ma.
But I don't really get down wit all that waiting in the lobby
for a nigga type shit, you feel me? When I'm ready to bless
you wit this dick again, I'll call you."

With that, Xavier left her standing there looking like a
fool as he exited through the hotel's revolving doors.

CHAPTER TWENTY ONE

Alaska

Alaska had her top down and her music blasting as she cruised up Spring Mountain in Omar's old BMW. She was listening to Jill Scott's new song "Blessed", and was singing along loudly to the track.

"Woke up this morning feelin' fresh to death I'm so blessed ... yes yes." Alaska sang getting into her groove. She heard her cell phone ringing and she picked it up and answered.

"Hello," Alaska answered, still snapping her fingers.

"What's up Alaska, its Jay."

"Oh, hey Jay, how are you?" she asked turning her music down. She hadn't talked to him since Andraya told her what went down. She was hoping he wasn't calling to talk about it because she didn't want to ruin her mood.

"I can't call it. Listen, I was calling to see if you ever got things rolling with Santee'."

"Um ... yeah, I did." Alaska replied, wondering where this was going. "Why do you ask?"

"'Cause it's time for me to get back in the game and I need to holla at him about it. You think you can setup a meeting for me?"

"I'll see what I can do. But are you sure you're ready for all that? I mean the game is pretty demanding, and you haven't even completed your physical therapy treatments yet." Alaska said, genuinely concerned.

"It's cool. I got Mo B reassembling the team as we speak. Once I have everybody on deck, I'll let them handle most of the dirty work while I just sit back and delegate shit."

"Well, I guess you got it all worked out then," Alaska chuckled. "Let me make a few phone calls and I'll get back with you, okay?"

"Bet. I really appreciate it, ma. I'll holla at 'chu later," Jay said before disconnecting the call.

Alaska made a left on Rainbow Boulevard and realized she wasn't too far from Santee's house. Since she needed to speak with him about a few things, she called to let him know she would be stopping by. Alaska pulled up to the six-thousand square foot Spanish style home, and parked the BMW in the circular cobblestone driveway right behind Santee's Cadillac XTS. When she got to the door she was greeted by his housekeeper, Mericella, who informed her that Santee' was in his study.

Alaska knocked softly on the oversized mahogany wood door before cracking it open and stepping inside.

"Hello, beautiful. And to what do I owe this wonderful pleasure," Santee' asked as he kissed Alaska on the cheek.

"Hey Santee'," she replied. "I just need to holla at you for a minute. But if I'm interrupting I can just get with you later," Alaska said noticing all the papers scattered across his desk.

"No, please, have a seat; it's no interruption at all. What can I do for you?"

"Thanks," Alaska smiled, taking a seat in one of the brown leather chairs, "I need to know where I can get a few guns from; preferably some untraceable ones."

Santee' was caught off guard, and he leaned back in his chair, folding his arms across his chest. "And what in the world would a pretty lady like you need guns for? Is somebody bothering you?"

"No, I'm fine," Alaska said, smiling at his concern, "But I'm ready to get at the nigga who murdered my husband, and I'm gonna need some heat in order to do it."

"I see" Santee' said, raising an eyebrow. "Well, I knew you were a pretty feisty woman, but I never pegged you for a killer."

"And I never thought I would be a drug dealer either, but here I am."

"Touché," Santee' replied. "So what's your plan?"

"My plan?" Alaska asked, not sure what he meant.

"Yeah, I mean, you're talking about murder here. You can't just walk up to the man and shoot him dead in the streets. You're gonna need some type of plan. Do you know where he lay his head? What kind of car he drive? Hell, do you even know his name?"

"Yes, yes and yes," Alaska replied, matter-of-factly. "I have all of that information and then some. I just haven't had time to sit down and formulate an exact plan yet."

Truthfully, Alaska hadn't even realized she needed a plan. Mo B had called her last night giving her everything he'd found out, she figured she could just use what he'd given her to catch Big Hank slipping.

"Listen; with all due respect love I don't think you're quite ready for this. Murder is a dirty game and if you're not careful, you could end up on the wrong side of the gun."

"So, what? I'm supposed to just let this nigga get away with killing the love of my life like everything is all gravy?" Alaska asked, catching an instant attitude. Santee' was coming at her as if she was naïve and incapable of getting the job done and she didn't appreciate it one bit.

"You know what, never mind. Just forget I asked. I'll find a way to get what I need on my own." Alaska snapped as she stood up to leave. But Santee' stopped her.

"Have a seat," he said sternly as he looked directly into her eyes. "Now listen, if you wanna go on a suicide mission and try to murk this man with no plan, then by all means, be my guest. But if you wanna dead that bastard and walk away with your life *and* your freedom, then you need to get up out of your feelings and let me help you do this the right way."

Alaska knew Santee' was right so instead of arguing, she just nodded her head in agreement. "So, what should I do then?"

"You should let me handle it. Omar was my man, and since I employ an entire team of men for situations just like this, it would be my honor to help you avenge his death. Men like Big Hank, who choose to rob and steal just to make a come up, are cowards in my book and I have no problem taking them out."

Alaska smiled. She had really wanted to be the one to get at Hank, but a part of her was relieved that she wouldn't have to do it all by herself. She was so relieved in fact, that it took a minute for all of Santee's words to fully register. When they did, her smile quickly faded.

"Wait a minute. How did you know his name?" Alaska asked, realizing she never said it during their conversation. For a split second Santee' seemed caught off guard, but he quickly recovered.

"The streets talk beautiful and it's my job to keep up with what their saying." Santee' smiled as he stood up and walked around to the front of his desk where Alaska was sitting. As he sat on the edge, Alaska got a whiff of his cologne and a flashback of his hands all over her body passed through her mind.

"If you already knew who killed him, why didn't you do anything?" Alaska asked, snapping out of her thoughts.

"It wasn't my battle to fight. The money and drugs stolen that night didn't belong to me, so it didn't make sense for me to start a war behind it."

"So why are you willing to start one now? I mean, what's changed?"

"You," Santee replied, as he stood up and pulled her in close. "I'm willing to do whatever it takes to make you happy and keep you safe. Murder is a man's job, and I could never forgive myself if I let you go out there and you end up getting hurt." Santee' ran his fingertips along the crook of Alaska's neck before lifting her chin and covering her lips with his.

The taste of his lips was sweet like honey, and Alaska wanted to stay lost in this moment forever. Just like that old R. Kelly song Bump and Grind, her mind was telling her no, but her body was telling her yes. Pulling away from his embrace, Alaska tried to regain her focus. Her emotions were all over the place when it came to Santee', and she didn't want to end up confusing her vulnerability with lust.

"I'm sorry," he said, realizing he'd crossed the line.

"It's okay," Alaska smiled weakly. "Well, I better get going. Thanks again for helping me out, I really appreciate it."

"It's no problem. Listen when you get a chance, I want you to go see an old friend of my mine. His name is Barry and he owns a gun shop over in Henderson. Since you're only getting deeper in the game, I wanna be sure you have some protection." Santee' grabbed a sticky note from his desk and wrote down the address to Barry's Gun Shop before handing it to Alaska, "Get whatever you want and tell him to charge it to my account, okay?"

Alaska took the bright yellow piece of paper and stuck it in her purse. "Thanks again, Sebastian."

"The pleasure is all mine," he smiled, as he watched her walk out the door.

Alaska was halfway to her car before she realized she'd forgotten to ask Santee' about meeting with Jay. *Oh well. If he wants to holla at Santee', I'll just tell him he's gotta go through me.*

Alaska climbed into her car and dropped the top as she pulled out of the driveway and sped away.

HEAVY

Alaska pulled into the valet outside of Caesars Palace and put her car in park. She was there to meet Sophia so that they could shop for their outfits for Santee's white party. As the valet attendant made his way over to her car, Alaska checked her hair and makeup in the mirror. Noticing that her lips looked a little dry, she applied more MAC lip gloss to them. When the valet opened her door, Alaska got out and handed him her keys plus a fifty dollar tip.

"Leave her up front for me, okay? I shouldn't be too long."

The attendant nodded and as Alaska looked up, she saw Sophia walking towards her.

"Perfect timing boo," Alaska said playfully as she reached out to give Sophia a hug.

"I know right. You ready to tear this mall up girl?

"Let's do it," Alaska said as they walked into the entrance of the Forum Shops. Since she preferred to start with her shoes, Alaska suggested they go into the Christian Louboutin store first. Even though it was an all white party, she planned to add some color and sparkle to her outfit with her choice of shoes and accessories.

"Ohh, look at these," Sophia said, holding up a pink pair of six inch Swarovski crystal encrusted stilettos.

"Those are cute, but I don't really do pink," Alaska replied as she eyed a pair of coral blue peep toe heels. "Now these, I like."

"Yeah, those are bad. And you can rock them with that blue Berkin bag I saw you carrying the other day. Add some gold accessories and you'll be good to go."

Alaska told the sales girl to bring her out a size 7 ½. . While they waited, the ladies browsed the rest of the store. When it was all said and done, both of them walked away with several pairs of shoes, spending more than eight thousand between them. The rest of their afternoon was filled with much of the same. The ladies tore through the mall throwing whatever they wanted in the bag and never once glanced at a price tag. By the time they made it to the Gucci store, Alaska had spent well over ten thousand on clothing, shoes and accessories. Having found her outfit for the party, as well as, two additional choices, she still couldn't stop herself from buying the fifteen hundred dollar white, one-shoulder cocktail dress that she saw hanging in the window.

"Girl, you gone be killin' 'em wit that one," Sophia said, as Alaska came out the dressing room modeling the dress.

"Yeah, I think this might be the one." Alaska said, turning around and looking over her shoulder to see how the dress looked from the back. She wished she still had the shopping bag with her shoes in it, but they had given all their purchases to the concierge to hold while they continued to shop.

"By the way, did you ever tell Santee' I was coming to the party?" Alaska asked. "I saw him earlier today, and he still didn't mention anything to me about it. I don't wanna show up and find out I wasn't really invited."

"Girl, boo," Sophia said, waving her hand dismissively. "You know good and damn well you're invited to that party. He probably just forgot to tell you. He's a pretty busy man you know."

Alaska gave herself a final once over before heading back into the dressing room to change. She knew Sophia was probably right, so she decided to go with the flow and disregarded the fact that she didn't have personal invitation from Santee'. Alaska paid for her purchases, and the ladies headed upstairs to the spa to get massages before ending their girl's day.

CHAPTER TWENTY TWO

Jay sat on the terrace of the nursing home, puffing on a blunt. It was just after midnight and the Las Vegas sky was clear and filled with stars. Jay stared at the full moon, and he wondered what Andraya was doing at this very moment. Not speaking to her the last few days was tearing him up inside and he didn't know how much more he could take. He understood she was upset, and rightfully so, but he just wanted her to give him a chance to apologize. He needed her to understand that he was just weak when it came to women, but it didn't mean he loved her any less.

For the hundredth time that day, Jay took his phone out of his pocket and dialed her number.

"Hey. You've reached…" Unable to listen to her voicemail greeting one more time, Jay hung up. Just as he was about to toss the phone over the balcony of the terrace in frustration, it rang.

"Hello!" Jay answered, hoping it was Draya.

"What's good fam?" Mo B asked on the other end of the phone. Jay was disappointed that it wasn't his wife, but he quickly regained his composure and flipped into business mode.

"What it do Mo B? What's the word?"

"I finally got the team together and we're all here at the warehouse. You want me to put you on speaker phone?"

"No not yet. Who's all there?" Jay questioned.

"Everybody 'cept Lil' Ray-Ray, Idris and Buddy. Dem niggas getting paper over there wit that nigga X, and they ain't tryna jump ship, you feel me? But the rest of us are all here, and we're ready to hear what you got to say. "

"Alright, cool. Put me on the speaker." Jay hadn't had a chance to talk to Alaska again, but he was still going to proceed as if he had. He knew she would be willing to do anything she could to help him out, so he wasn't worried about her not coming through on his meeting request.

"Gentlemen, it's good to speak with all of you again," Jay said into the phone. "I want to start by thanking all of you for coming out. I know there's been a lot of talk and speculation in regards to my whereabouts, but as all of you can hear, I'm alive and well. But unfortunately, my cousin Omar wasn't so lucky, and that's why I called this meeting. I've decided to keep things going and pick up where he left off. I need everybody that's still down to resume their old positions. When the first shipment comes down the pipe, I need y'all to be ready. Mo B; I need you to hold down the eastside spots since Idris and Buddy are gone. Tae' and Rock; I need y'all to grab Ray Ray's old territory on the westside."

With everybody versed on what they needed to do, Jay told Mo B he would hit him back once he got the product. Before he disconnected the call, Jay also gave Mo B the co-ordinates to the nursing facility and told him to be there to-morrow morning at eight o'clock. Even though he hadn't completed his therapy, Jay decided tonight would be his last night calling the facility home. With his marriage falling apart and his pockets on E, he knew it was time for him to go home and get his house back in order. As he made his way back to his room, Jay heard a familiar voice as he came upon the nurses' station. When he turned his wheelchair around the corner, he saw his wife standing there looking more beautiful than ever in a flowing yellow BCBG maxi dress. Her long black hair was pulled back into a sleek ponytail, and her flawless chocolate colored skin was glowing without even the slightest hint of makeup.

At that moment, Jay would have given anything to be able to walk over and pull his wife into his arms. He was yearning to touch her, feel her, and smell her just like he used to do before everything went left.

"Draya," he called out to get her attention. When she saw him, she ended her conversation with the nurse and walked over to him.

"Hey," was all she said, as her eyes shifting nervously around the room.

"I didn't expect to see you here. Why haven't you been answering any of my calls?"

"Cause I needed time to think," Draya said, letting out a huge sigh. "Look, can we go in your room so we can talk in private, please?"

Jay nodded as he led the way down the hall to his room. Once inside, Draya reached into her purse and re-trieved a large manila envelope, handing it to Jay.

"I didn't want to have you served because I didn't want to run the risk of someone finding out where you were."

"What is it?" Jay asked, lifting the two silver tabs to unseal the envelope and slowly pulling out the papers that were inside. The words "Dissolution of Marriage", with him and Draya's names both typed underneath, stared back at him.

"I'm not asking for any money or spousal support," Draya said nervously, "and you can even keep the house and both of cars. The only thing I want from you is your signa-ture on those papers, and the promise that you won't make this any harder than it has to be."

Jay looked up at his wife in disbelief. "You can't be se-rious."

"As a heart attack."

"But you haven't even given me a chance to explain."

"What is there to explain, Jay? I saw you butt naked with your dick inside another bitch's pussy. I think that visual was explanation enough."

"Baby," Jay whispered, as he reached out to touch her hand. He knew she was upset, but he never dreamed she would actually file for divorce without at least speaking to him first. "Baby, please don't leave me. Give me a chance and I promise I'll make it up to you. I'll do whatever it takes; just don't walk away from me, Draya. I need you, ma."

Draya looked down at Jay with tears in her eyes. Even though she made up her mind to leave a long time ago, it still pained her see the hurt and sadness in Jay's eyes.

"I can't," she said, pulling her hand away from his grasp. "Too much has gone down, and I'm just not happy anymore. I love you, Jay, and I always will. But I have to go."

Draya leaned down and kissed him softly on the check. At the same time, she used her foot to set the safety lock on his wheelchair preventing him from coming after her as she walked away.

"Goodbye, Jay."

Draya placed her wedding ring on the bedside table and walked out the door. Determined to stop her, Jay stood up from his wheelchair and took three steps before collapsing to the ground.

"FUCK!" he yelled as he pounded the cold linoleum floor. Nothing, not even the five shots he endured during the robbery, could compare to the pain he felt in his heart at that very moment.

Unable to move, Jay would lay there until Mo B arrived to take him home.

CHAPTER TWENTY THREE

Xavier

Xavier drove the Buick Regal he'd just stolen, into a quiet subdivision and parked it on the curb. He'd just left a meeting with his girl Yvette, where he learned that she was unable to get the coordinates to the facility that Jay was in. She did however, obtain the name and address of Sharonda Fatty, a nurse who was just fired from the facility for having an improper relationship with one of her patients.

"Well I guess it's time to pay Ms. Fatty a little visit then." Xavier smiled as he took the address from Yvette.

"And what if she doesn't bite?"

"I got ten thousand stacks that guarantee she will."

"What if it's not that easy? The people who run that facility have gone to great lengths to keep its location a secret. The money you're offering probably pales in comparison to what those people will do to her."

Xavier thought about Yvette's words as he climbed out of the car and walked up the sidewalk. He really didn't want to kill the girl, so he was hoping the cash inside his backpack would do the trick. But as he walked up to the modest, two story home Xavier attached the silencer to the end of his gun just in case. He removed the black hoodie he'd worn to cover his face on the walk over from the car, and he shook his dreads out until they fell evenly onto his shoulders. It was late and he didn't want to appear to menacing, so Xavier put on a pair of black framed reading glasses and made sure the modest gold Jesus piece he was wearing was visible also. Standing on her doorstep, he reached out to ring the doorbell but to his surprise it swung open.

"Who the fuck is you," Sharonda slurred. She answered the door wearing nothing but a pair of black shorts which looked more like panties, and a pink wife-beater. Xavier noticed she was holding a bottle of Remy White in her right hand, and a freshly rolled blunt in her left. *This might be easier than I thought,* he said to himself. Taking note of her inebriated state, he also noticed how fine she was as his eyes roamed all over her body.

"Uh, hello muthafucka," Sharonda said waving her hands in his face to get his attention. "Nigga, I said who the fuck is you?"

"Damn, ma. You got a foul ass mouth, you know that?"

"I beg yo pardon? How the fuck you gone come up on my porch at one o'clock in the damn morning and try to tell me how the fuck to talk? Ain't that some shit?"

Xavier couldn't help but to smile. "Okay ma. You got that," he said putting his hands up in surrender. He could tell she was a feisty one, and her attitude sort of turned him on. "My name is X, and I came here because I have a proposition for you."

"What kind of proposition?"

"The kind that can make you a lot of money," Xavier said, adjusting the backpack on his shoulder.

"As long as it doesn't involve sex; I don't fuck niggas I don't know."

Xavier chuckled, "I promise there's absolutely no sex involved, ma. Unless of course, you tryna get to know a nigga." He licked his lips and turned his mouth up into a seductive grin.

"Cute," Sharonda said sarcastically as she opened the door a litter wider. "Come on in."

HEAVY

As they walked down the narrow hallway that led to the living room, Xavier was able to get a perfect view of her backside. *Damn!* He thought as he watched the tiny black shorts she wore disappear in between her massive ass cheeks with each step.

"You can have a seat. I'm gonna go make me another drink and I'll be right back. You want something?"

"Yeah, make me one of whatever you're having," Xavier said as took a seat on the couch. He wasn't sure why he felt so relaxed around her, but he did. Maybe it was her around the way girl attitude, or maybe it was the fact that she seemed to feel just as comfortable around him. Either way, if everything went the way he planned, he was definitely going to try and see her again so he could smash that ass.

"So, let me guess," Sharonda said, returning with their drinks, "you're a reporter and you wanna be the first one to finally get some information on the facility, right?"

"What? Uh ... yeah, you're right. I work for The Sun," Xavier said playing it off. "How did you know?"

"It's only been a week since they fired me, and you're the sixth muthafucka to show up on my doorstep unannounced and asking questions. Plus, the nerdy glass, backpack and that small ass chain you're rocking gave it all away."

Sharonda chuckled at her own joke before she continued, "But unfortunately sweetheart, Imma have to tell you like I told all of them; I ain't got shit for ya. The muthafuckas that own that place don't take to kindly to bitches running their mouths. And even though shit in my life ain't all that great right now, I'd still like to keep living it. So sorry, but I can't be a part of your story boo-boo."

"But you ain't even heard my offer yet ma. I'm not asking for personal quotes or any behind the scenes scandalous shit, I only need one thing and I'm willing to pay you pretty swell for it."

Sharonda paused. None of the other reporters who showed up on her doorstep ever mentioned anything about money. Hell, if they had she would've been on an island somewhere sipping Mojitos instead of standing here talking to Xavier.

"How much you talkin'," Sharonda asked curiously.

There was only had ten thousand dollars in his back-pack, but as Xavier looked around Sharonda's newly built and well decorated home, he knew he would have to raise the stakes in order to make it worth her while.

"Fifty thousand dollars; I'll give you ten of it right now," he said patting the backpack, "and the remainder once I verify the information you give me is legit."

"Okay. What do you wanna know?"

"The coordinates," Xavier replied, plain and simple.

"That's it?" Sharonda asked, as if giving up that information wasn't an automatic death sentence. She stood up to retrieve a pen and a piece of paper on which she wrote a series of numbers before handing it to Xavier.

"The facility's location is off the grid so those coordinates will only get you to a certain point. Once you reach it, you'll still have to drive about fifteen miles on a dark road surrounded by nothing but trees and wild animals. It's kinda like driving through the rainforest or some shit," Sharonda nervously chuckled. "I have a map that they gave me when I first starting working there which shows the rest of the route. Let me go grab it for you cause trust me, you don't wanna get lost out there in that bullshit."

Xavier was so shocked at how easily she gave up the information that he just nodded his head in agreement. He watched as she disappeared down the hallway and into her bedroom, closing the door softly behind her.

As soon as Sharonda entered the room, a huge smile spread across her face as she grabbed her cell phone off the dresser. As she strolled through her contacts, her heart began to race and her palms got sweaty thinking about the big pay-day she was about to receive. Although the fifty thousand dollars Xavier was offering was a nice come up, the two hundred and fifty grand she would get for turning his ass in to the officials at the facility was even nicer. Initially, when Sharonda seen Xavier standing at her front door she thought he was there for her little sister, Saamala, who was temporally living with her until she got on her feet. But it didn't take her long to realize he was there looking for her, and when he mentioned that he had a proposition, she knew instantly that her plan had worked.

    Three years ago, when she first started working at the facility, Sharonda had been so excited to finally have a job that she eagerly signed the confidentiality agreement they presented to her with no questions asked. It wasn't until she came across the papers while cleaning out her closet the day after she was fired, that she decided to actually look them over. To her surprise, there was a clause in the agreement that allowed any employee, past or present, to collect a re-ward of up to $250,000 for reporting any persons trying to gain information on the facility for any reason. Faced with the reality of living off the tiny ass unemployment check she was granted from the state, Sharonda instantly made a deci-sion to use the clause to her advantage.

    Anonymously, she sent letters to the head writers of every major newspaper in the surrounding area and provided them with a "tip" on her connection to the facility. Since the names of all employees at the facility were kept top secret and pretty much impossible for the public to obtain. Sharonda knew it wouldn't be long before some young, bright eyed writer itching to impress his boss, showed up at her door. But that was hardly the case. Although she'd told Xavier he was one of many to show up at her door, truthfully, he was the first. After three whole days and not one single call, Sharonda had given up on her get rich quick scheme and resorted to smoking and drinking her days away.

But now with Xavier waiting in her living room, she was finally ready to collect on her big payday. She hit the send button on her Blackberry and listened as the phone rang on the other line.

"Please enter your access code and press the pound key," stated the recording. Sharonda typed in the five digit code listed on the agreement.

"One moment, please." A series of clicks followed and then a woman's voice came on the line. "This is Jane. How may I help you?"

"Yeah, Jane. How you doing? My name is Sharonda Fatty. I'm a former employee there, and I was calling to report ..."

POP! POP! POP!

Before Sharonda could say another word the bullets from Xavier's .38 pierced through her head, leaving her permanently speechless.

Dumb bitch, Xavier thought as he watched a pool of blood surround her body.

He knew Sharonda's willingness to give up the information so fast was suspect, so it didn't surprise him when Yvette sent him a text message telling him to abort the mission. Through one of her many connections, she'd found out about the clause in the agreement, as well as, the letters Sharonda had sent to all the newspapers, and she alerted Xavier immediately. Before making his exit, he stopped in the living room to retrieve the glass he'd been drinking out of, and he made sure he didn't leave anything else behind. Once he was out of the house and back in his car, Xavier sent Yvette a text that simply read, *Good lookin.*

As he quietly pulled out of the subdivision, Xavier typed the coordinates Sharonda had given him into his GPS system. If they were correct, tonight was gonna be Jay's last night breathing.

CHAPTER TWENTY FOUR

Andraya

Andraya removed her Gucci shades as she walked through the entrance of the downtown medical building. Studying the directory on the wall, she saw that the office of Dr. Michael Shoeman was on the fifth floor so she made her way across the room to the elevators. Once inside, Andraya took a deep breath. Last night, after the realization that she'd just served her husband with divorce papers hit her like a ton of bricks, her sister Carmen called with one last plea to help save their mother's life. With the guilt of ending her marriage weighing heavily on her shoulders, Draya finally gave in and agreed to get tested. Carmen had been so happy on the other end of the phone that it instantly made Draya smile. She hadn't heard her sister's laughter in over six years, and the sound warmed her heart.

The two of them proceeded to talk for more than three hours as they caught each other up on what's been going on in their lives. Although Draya enjoyed the conversation with her sister, it felt bittersweet because she couldn't really tell Carmen about everything that's been going on. She couldn't mention the fact that her husband was almost killed in drug deal gone wrong, or that she was now leaving him due to the injuries and loss of status he'd sustained from it. Nor could Draya tell her that she was now back in the arms of the true

8

love of her life, Xavier. Revealing those truths would have indubitably taken their relationship twenty steps back, so Draya held them in. As their conversation ended, Draya agreed to meet Carmen the next morning at the medical building downtown.

But now, as Draya walked through the glass doors of the doctor's office, a feeling of fear entered into her spirit. What if she was actually a match? Had she forgiven her mother and sister enough to actually go through with the surgery? Would they still accept her back into their lives once they found out she was back with Xavier? The fear of rejection made Draya want to walk right back out the door, but her plan was stalled when she was spotted by the receptionist.

"Hello. Can I help you?" the woman asked pulling back the glass window that separated them.

"Umm ... no I ..."

"Hey sis," Carmen cut Draya off mid-sentence as she strolled through the door and hugged her tight.

"Morning, Jade," Carmen greeted the receptionist. "This is my sister Andraya. She's here to get tested to see if she's a match for mom's kidney."

"Well hello, Andraya. I've heard so much about you. It's so nice to finally meet you. Let me tell Dr. Shoeman you guys are here. Make yourselves comfortable and he should be out in a minute."

Draya smiled nervously as she watched the petite older woman disappear around the corner.

"Sorry I'm late," Carmen said as she took a seat in one of the waiting room chairs. "I had to get LiL Malcolm and Mariah off to school."

"Oh, it's okay. I just got here myself."

"You know, Malcolm and the kids really want to meet you. If you're not busy, you should stop by for dinner one day this week. I'll even make a chocolate punch bowl cake just for you."

Draya smiled at the mention of their favorite childhood dessert.

"I would love that. Just let me know what day and time, and I'll be there."

Draya took a seat next to her sister and looked around the nicely decorated waiting room. She made note of the plush carpet, expensive furniture and collectable art that lined the walls. While almost everything in Las Vegas could be considered over the top, this was the first time Draya had been in doctor's office that was this fancy. The waiting room also had a fireplace with a sixty inch flat screen TV mounted above it.

The volume on the TV was muted, but the headline on the screen caught Draya's attention.

SHOOTING AT PRIVATE REHABILITATION CENTER LEAVES ONE DEAD.

"Can you turn that up?" Draya asked the receptionist as she walked over and stood directly in front of the TV.

"Reports are coming in at this hour that a shooting has occurred at a private rehab center frequented by celebrities and high ranking political figures. At this time, authorities have not released the victim's name, nor have they given the name and location of the facility. Stay tuned to Local 5 News as we continue to bring you the latest on this breaking news story. I'm Chris Thomas, signing out."

Draya's heart fell to her feet. "Oh my God, they found him."

"Found who?" Carmen asked, suddenly appearing at her side. Draya didn't realize she had been speaking out loud until she looked up and saw that all eyes were on her.

"I'm sorry, but I gotta go," she said grabbing her bag.

"But, what about the test?" Carmen asked frantically as Draya made a beeline for the door.

"Reschedule it," she answered as nicely as she could before stepping onto the elevator. What Draya really wanted to say was *fuck you and that damn test*, but since the two of them had just gotten back on speaking terms, she didn't want to ruin their progress.

Draya's cell phone couldn't pick up any service on the elevator, but the moment she stepped foot outside the reception returned. She quickly hit the number two key which was programmed to speed dial the facility and she waited for someone to pick up.

"Hi, this is Tasha. How may I help you?"

"Yes, this is Andraya Montgomery, Jay Montgomery's wife. Can I be connected to his room please?" Draya was too afraid to just come out and ask if her husband had been the victim in the shooting, so she just asked to be connected to his room instead.

"Sure," the receptionist answered in a bubbly tone. "I'll just need you to provide me with his code."

"7415."

Draya began to breathe a sigh of relief as she rattled off the personal security code used to identify her as a member of Jay's family.

"Thank you. One moment please," the young girl sang.

Judging by the annoyingly chipper tone in the receptionist's voice, Draya was starting to think that everything must be okay. *If not, then why the hell is she so fuckin' happy,* Draya thought.

Convincing herself that everything was alright, Draya was just about to hang up the phone when she heard a different female voice come back on the line.

"Hello, Mrs. Montgomery?"

"Yes."

"Umm ... I apologize Mrs. Montgomery, but it appears that your husband is no longer with us."

Her words hit Draya like a Mack truck, causing her to bring her car to a complete stop in the middle of the expressway. Their relationship might have been over, but Draya didn't wish death on any one.

Tears began to stream down her face and cars whizzed by her honking their horns as she sat in the driver's seat of the car unable to move.

CHAPTER TWENTY FIVE

Xavier

Xavier handed Andraya a cup of tea as he took a blanket and gently wrapped it around her shoulders. Although she didn't know it, Xavier knew her call would be coming as soon as she found out that Jay had been killed. So he made sure he had everything in place to help comfort her when she did. Although what he was doing was wrong, Xavier didn't feel bad because it was what he was forced to do in order to survive. If he didn't get the payment that was owed to him for doing the job, Xavier would be stuck out here with no way to support himself. His mother kept telling him she could put in a good word with her manager down at the phone company where she worked, but Xavier just reminded her every time she mentioned it that he wasn't about that life. Working a 9 to 5 and punching some white man's clock was not his idea of living. Xavier wanted to the feel the rush that only being a dope boy could give, and he was determined to make it happen again.

"Now tell me what happened," Xavier said softly to Andraya now that he'd finally gotten her to calm down.

"I was at the doctor's office when I seen a clip on the news detailing a shooting that happened last night at the facility where Jay was staying. Not knowing what was going on, I left my appointment and jumped in my car to head over there. On the way I called and asked to speak with him and that's when the lady told me he was no longer with us."

A tear slid down Draya's cheek as she repeated the woman's words. Part of her was saddened that Jay was gone, but the other part of her was just as relieved that he was. Now she would be able to get on with her life without feeling any guilt or dealing with any divorce drama. But, the icing on the cake was going to be the three million dollar life insurance policy Draya stood to collect once everything was all said and done. Draya had taken the policy out days after Jay was shot the first time and nobody, not even Jay, knew about its existence.

"I'm sorry to hear that ma." Xavier put his arm around Draya and pulled her in close. He genuinely felt sorry for her and he wished for the millionth time that their circumstances had been different. "You can stay here as long as you want, and I promise everything will be okay."

"Thank you Xavier," Draya replied as she leaned her head back on his chest.

Looking for something to lighten the mood, Xavier grabbed the remote control and turned on the TV. Ironically, Andraya's favorite episode of the old TV show Martin was on. She began to laugh immediately when she saw Martin and his girlfriend Gina, fighting the big ass rat that had taken over their hotel room while on their vacation to "Cilligan's Island".

"This used to be my favorite show." Draya said cracking up.

"Mine too!"

Just as Martin was starting to get the best of the rat, Xavier's cell phone rang. Looking down at the caller ID, Xavier excused himself and took the call in his bedroom so he wouldn't bother Andraya.

As she sat there laughing, Draya remembered watching the show every Thursday night with her family and the memory made her feel good. When the show went to commercial, Draya was about to go to the kitchen for more tea when she saw the words breaking news strolled across the TV. Frozen in her tracks, Draya listened as the same news anchor from earlier came on to give an update on the situation.

"Good Evening. I'm Chris Thomas, coming to you again tonight with an update on that shooting at a private rehab center outside of Las Vegas. The brazen killing appears to be a hit and the police have confirmed the identity of the victim as that of a thirty-nine year old Nevada senator Kevin Blackwood. Mr. Blackwood had just checked into the facility last night to seek treatment for injuries he suffered in a car accident last month, and authorities don't believe he was the intended target. Instead they believe the target was the man who occupied Mr. Blackwood's room only hours before he was checked in. Police have not released that man's name to the public, but they do state that he is wanted for questioning. As always, be sure to stay tuned to Local 5 News for further updates on this and other important stories. I'm Chris Thomas, signing out. "

Andraya was shocked by the report and she quickly rushed to the back of the condo to tell Xavier what she'd just saw. But Draya was frozen in her tracks again as she reached the bedroom and heard Xavier's voice. She peeked through the crack in the door and saw him standing there with his phone to his ear watching the very same newscast she just walked away from.

"I can't believe this shit," Xavier spat. "How the fuck did I let this happen?"

"Because your ass is incompetent that's why," yelled the other voice on the end of the phone. "I sent you in there to do one thing and you can't even get that shit right. Why the fuck didn't you verify that it was that nigga before you even left.

"I didn't have enough time," Xavier said pissed off that he had failed again. "A nurse in a nearby room heard the shots and called for an immediate lockdown of the facility. I had to hurry up and get out of there or risk being caught."

Andraya's heart was beating out of her chest as she listened to Xavier's words. Now his sudden reappearance into her life didn't seem so random. Draya realized his plan had been to use her just to get next to Jay all along.

"Let me try again," Xavier pleaded as he shut the TV off.

"Naw. Watching you fail one time was more than enough. Your services will no longer be needed." The caller hung up and Xavier hurled his phone across the room in frustration.

Not ready to confront him with what she heard, Andraya ran back to the living room and took her place back on the couch. When Xavier came out of the room she acted as if she hadn't heard a thing.

"Everything alright?" she asked as he walked over and turned off the TV.

"Yeah, everything's cool. Listen, why don't we get out of here and go get something to eat. I'm starving," Xavier said nervously as he wiped the sweat from his brow. He needed to get her away from the TV for a minute while he tried to figure this shit out.

"Sure," Draya said as she stood up smiling like nothing was wrong. "I'm starving too. Let's go."

Xavier suggested that they go to her favorite soul food restaurant, Big Mama's Kitchen, and Andraya happily agreed. The ride over was quiet as both of them became too lost in their own thoughts to worry about the other. Andraya was hurt by what she'd just learned, but still the betrayal wasn't enough to make her walk away. Instead, she decided in that moment that she would reverse the tables and use Xavier to get the only thing she ultimately wanted anyway; money. As they continued down Rainbow Blvd, Draya mapped out exactly what she was going to say once they made it to the restaurant.

Xavier sat next to Andraya in the driver's seat of his Benz, pissed off. He couldn't believe he failed at his only shot to get back on, and now he had no idea what he was going to do. If Big Hank wasn't coughing up that fifty thousand dollars, then he might as well take his mother up on her offer and apply for a job down at the phone company.

"FUCK!" Xavier yelled as he banged his fist on the steering wheel. He had forgotten Andraya was in the car until she spoke.

"What's the matter?" she asked looking over at him strangely.

"Nothing, I just forgot my phone," he lied. He tried counting to ten to help him calm down, but that shit wasn't working. Everything was falling apart and he had no idea what he was going to do now.

CHAPTER TWENTY SIX

When Jay heard the shots pop off at the rehab facility on his way out the door, he was glad that he had changed his mind and told Mo B to pick him up then instead of in the morning. His intuition was telling him that Big Hank was going to eventually come back and finish the job; last night had likely been the night. As he sat on the couch in the apartment Vanessa shared with her mother, Jay watched the news broadcast about the shooting and he wondered why Andraya hadn't even bothered to call. Major news outlets like CNN and MSNBC had picked up on the story, and social media was even going crazy sharing it so Jay knew she had to have heard about it by now. Yet he still hadn't heard from her and he was vexed. Since he couldn't go home, Jay came to the only place where he knew no one would expect him to be.

Now seven months pregnant, Vanessa came waddling over to him with a freshly rolled blunt and Heineken in her hand. "Here you go baby," she smiled handing Jay the items as she sat back down next to him. She was so happy to see him alive again that she didn't want to let him out of her sight.

"Thanks," Jay replied taking a swig of the already opened beer. He grabbed a lighter from off the table and lit the blunt. He took the first hit and held it in his lungs for a moment before blowing it out his nose.

HEAVY

"Don't you need to be going in the other room or something?" Jay asked looking over at Vanessa. "I'm pretty sure inhaling weed smoke ain't good for the baby."

"Oh, right." Vanessa replied embarrassed that she hadn't thought of that herself. She had been so wrapped up in Jay's presence that she wasn't thinking.

"I'll be back in the bedroom if you need me."

Jay didn't even bother to help her as she struggled to get up off the couch, and Vanessa rolled her eyes at him when she finally stood up and started to walk away.

"Aye," Jay called out to her before she made it too far. "Why don't you do me a favor and go get me something to eat instead. I got a taste for some of that catfish from the BBQ place around the corner."

"I would baby, but the car's not here."

"So," Jay replied taking another pull of the blunt.

"So how the hell am I supposed to get there Jay?" Vanessa asked as she coped and attitude and put her hands up on her hips.

"Walk," Jay said simply. "It's good for the baby and you could use the exercise anyway."

Vanessa stood there with her mouth open in shock as Jay turned around and returned his attention to the TV. She couldn't believe how disrespectful this nigga was being. If she had of been one of those bum bitches that didn't care if their kid grew up without a father, she probably would have killed Jay her damn self.

"Well are you at least going to give me some money?" Vanessa asked incredulously.

"Nope," Jay said without even turning around.

Vanessa was so angry that when she slammed the door on her way out, she made the walls shake and several of her mother's pictures dropped to the ground.

"Oh my God he is such a fucking asshole," Vanessa said out loud as she stepped in to the scorching Las Vegas summer heat. It had to be at least a hundred degrees outside and she couldn't believe he was making her walk two whole blocks just to get his greedy ass something to eat. Nor could she believe she was actually doing the shit. It must have been the power of love Vanessa concluded as she started sweating bullets fifteen seconds into her trek. By the time she made it to the popular restaurant she felt like she was about to have a heat stroke. When Vanessa walked through the door she felt the cool burst of central air hit her body and she breathed a sigh of relief.

Sitting down to catch her breath, Vanessa briefly locked eyes with the cutie sitting one booth over. As she registered his face, she thought that she knew him from somewhere but she couldn't remember where it was. Dismissing the thought, Vanessa relaxed a few more minutes before she got up and went to the register to place her order. When she made her way back to the booth to wait for her food, she looked a little closer at the dude occupying the booth over from hers and this time she saw that Andraya was there too. *That's where I know his ass from,* Vanessa thought as she remembered seeing Draya and the dude chilling together a few times around town.

Back then, Vanessa was under the impression that Jay was dead so she didn't make much of it. But now that she knew he had been alive this whole time, she knew that Draya had been cheating on Jay and she couldn't wait to get back home to spill the beans. As Vanessa thanked God for the all the good fortune that had come into her life over the last twenty-four hours; finding out Jay was still alive and now this, she leaned in closer to ensure that she was able to hear every word.

CHAPTER TWENTY SEVEN

Andraya

Draya took the macaroni and cheese that was stuck to the end of her folk and dipped it in the pool of barbeque sauce that had formed underneath her ribs, but she never ate it. Instead she just continued to drag the fork across her plate mixing everything together like a four year old kid.

"What's wrong? You don't like it?" Xavier asked when he noticed she wasn't eating.

"No, it's not that," Andraya said taking a deep breath. She knew once the words she was about to speak fell from her mouth she would never be able to put them back in. She paused to ask herself if this was what she really wanted. Positive that it was, she looked Xavier in the eyes before she continued.

"I overheard your phone call back at the house." She informed him. "Jay is still alive and I know that you're the person who tried to kill him."

Xavier slowly stopped chewing as he sat the rib he'd been eating back down on his plate. He grabbed his napkin and Draya could see the wheels turning in his head as he tried to come up with a response to what she'd just said.

"I'm sorry Draya. I didn't want to hurt you but I really needed the money. Ever since I got out..."

"Save it," Draya said putting up her hand as she cut him off. "I let you play me once, but now things have changed. Unless you want me to call Jay right now and tell him where he can find you, then we're going to start to play this game by my rules."

Xavier didn't respond at first. Instead his just folded his arms and laid them against chest as he sat back in the chair. "Go on," he finally said.

"First, I need to know the whereabouts of the man who hired you." Draya demanded.

"I can't give you that information."

"You can and you will," she said reaching for her phone. "Or I will hit send on this message and within five minutes, twenty trigger happy goons will ascend on this bitch like fly on shit. Your choice."

Xavier was vexed. He hated that he was being punked by a bitch, but his back was up against the wall. He only had one strap and no men on his team, so it would be foolish to try and go up against Jay's army. Besides, Hank had played him by not giving him another chance to finish the job so Xavier said fuck it.

"His name is Big Hank, but that's just his street name. I don't know his real one. He lives in L.A but he's here in Vegas all the time. The directions to his house are in my GPS; I can give them to you when we go back to the car," Xavier offered.

"Where does he lay his head when he's here in Vegas?" Draya asked.

"Usually at the Palazzo or the Wynn."

"Does he travel with goons?" Andraya needed to know exactly how Hank moved.

"Naw, that nigga's too reckless to move that smart. He let the little come up he made off the robbery gas him up and now he thinks he's Mr. Untouchable. But the nigga's got a nasty cocaine habit and he's addicted to bitches, so if you trying to get at him, I'm sure it wouldn't be that hard."

"Good enough," Draya said committing the information to her memory. She felt bad about what she was about to do. But she felt that getting the 411 on Hank and giving it to Alaska would somehow make her betrayal a little lighter.

"Secondly, I want you to try it again. But this time, I need you to *actually* kill my husband." The sound of a glass breaking came from behind them, but Draya was too in the zone to turn around and see what was going on.

"What? You're not serious," Xavier said searching her face to see if she was joking.

"Does it look like I'm joking?" Andraya's face remained stoned, and Xavier sat back and looked at her in amazement. He couldn't believe how she had flipped the script that fast. Less than an hour ago she was a grieving wife. Now that she knew he was still alive, she was sitting here ordering his murder. *What part of the game is this,* Xavier thought.

"If I do it, what do I get out of it?" he asked. Xavier just needed to get paid, and at this point he was willing to do whatever it took.

"I'll give you whatever Hank was paying you. But truthfully you don't even deserve that. You betrayed me for the second time and you should just be grateful that I'm letting you walk away with your life."

Xavier nodded his head in agreement. He had never seen this bossy side of Draya before and he had to admit it was hella sexy. Even though she just threatened to have him killed, he still had an urge to reach over the table and tongue her down.

"How much was he paying you?" Draya asked, snapping Xavier out of his thoughts.

"One hundred stacks."

"I'll give you fifty," Draya replied, knowing he'd doubled the price.

"Cool." Xavier agreed. Andraya grabbed her purse and started to stand up from the table but he stopped her.

"Wait. What about us?" he asked grabbing her arm.

"What about us?" Draya said snatching back her arm as she stood up. "I'm going to catch a cab home. Make sure you stay ready 'cause we're going to move soon. I'll call you later on with the details."

With that, Draya pulled her Gucci shades down over her eyes and walked out of the restaurant.

CHAPTER TWENTY EIGHT

Alaska

Alaska checked the mirror to make sure that her hair and makeup were perfect one last time before she walked out of the bathroom. She finally agreed to let Santee' take her out and tonight had been their first official date. They painted the town red, enjoying dinner at a rooftop restaurant followed by a helicopter ride over The Strip and the Grand Canyon. Now they were back at Santee's house for a nightcap, and Alaska realized that for the first time she didn't feel guilty being alone with him. Alaska's five inch heels clicked along the marble floor as she walked back to the living room where Santee' was waiting. When she entered, she was surprised to find the lights dimmed and candles flickering around the room as Santee' stood in the middle of it.

"Come here," he beckoned, holding his hand out for her. Slowly Alaska walked over to him taking everything in. Omar had always made her feel special throughout their relationship, but very few times had she ever felt like she did tonight. Santee' had a way about him that just pulled her in and made her feel safe. Even when she wanted to run, something about the sound of his voice and the touch of his hand convinced her to stay. He was giving her the one thing she never thought she would find again after Omar died and that was love.

When Alaska got close enough, she put her hand into his and Santee' gently pulled her into his space. He gazed into her eyes as the two of them stood just inches apart and he whispered, "You're beautiful," before covering his lips with hers. Alaska melted into his arms as she fully surrendered to the feelings she'd been fighting much too long. She feverishly kissed him back as Santee' grabbed the back of her head pressing their lips even closer together. It had been months since Alaska felt the power of a man between her thighs, and her entire body was tingling with anticipation as she thought of what was to come.

Like a scene out of a movie, Santee' clapped his hands and Robin Thicke's "Sex Therapy" came floating through the room's built in speakers. Alaska chuckled to herself as she wondered if that had been planned. Santee' guided her over to the fireplace where he pushed one of the many buttons that was on the wall. Instantly, a section of the marble floor retracted and out popped a platform with a king size bed on top of it.

"Impressive," Alaska smiled as she ran her fingers through his hair. "Do you do this for all of your women, or am I just special?" she said playfully.

"Only for you, ma. And trust me when I tell you love, you're one of the most special women I have ever had the pleasure of meeting."

"Is that so?" Alaska asked as she removed her shoes and crawled to the center of the bed. "Then why don't you come over here and show me just how special I *really* am."

Santee' didn't need her to say it twice as he quickly removed his shoes and climbed into the bed. Instantly the two of them began to hungrily feed off one another as they took turns sucking, pulling kissing, and licking every part of each other's body. The feeling was like a torture chamber of pleasure and Alaska's head began to spin as she experienced pure euphoria. By the time Santee's mouth found its way to her center, Alaska was dripping like a river and the sheets underneath her were soaking wet.

"Damn ma. This is the wettest pussy I've ever seen," Santee' said as she slowly began to lap up her juices. Her creamy filling was sweet like coconut milk and he couldn't get enough of it as he dined on her like she was his last meal.

"Ohhh shit... yeah daddy, right there." Alaska moaned as he flicked his tongue over her spot.

"You like that shit baby?" Santee' spoke as he happily fulfilled her request.

"Yes Santee'! I love it papi!"

The sound of her calling out his name sent Santee' into overdrive and he sucked and licked her clit until cum squirted from her middle.

"OH SHIT PAPI! YESSSSSSSS!" Alaska released months' worth of sexual frustration all over Santee's face and he loved every second of it. Alaska was spent as she laid there trying to catch her breath. She wanted to return the favor and bless him with a taste of her impeccable head game, but before she could even get up the energy, Santee' was on top of her. He left kisses on the crook of her neck before softly biting down on her earlobe as he whispered, "Alaska Drake, may I please have the pleasure of making love to you?"

Alaska's heart turned to mush. If she hadn't already been sure about giving herself to Santee', his words had just solidified it now.

"Yes," she answered breathlessly.

The moment he entered her body, Alaska's pussy muscle contracted around his dick and she found herself cuming again for the second time. Santee' held her as she moaned out in pleasure and trembled in his arms. When she was finished, Santee' proceeded to make love to her in a way that Alaska had never before experienced. By the time it was all said and done, Alaska came five more times before Santee' finally released his load inside of her womb.

As the two of them laid there in a sex induced utopia, Alaska prayed that the feeling would never end. Too tired to move, the two of them fell asleep in front of the fireplace, wrapped in each other's arms.

The next morning, Alaska awoke to the sound of heels clicking against the floor. As she blinked her eyes trying to adjust them to the light, she saw Sophia standing over the bed with her hand on her hip.

"And what do we have here?" Sophia said as she glaring down at Alaska, "Looks like somebody's trying to fuck her way to the top, huh girls?"

Alaska sat up realizing Sophia wasn't alone. When she saw Daphne and Kim standing in the doorway along with one of Santee's male workers, she became totally embarrassed and she pulled the sheet up higher around her body.

"Listen, I'm sorry," Alaska said feeling like she needed to apologize for some reason.

"You ain't got to be sorry, honey. What you do with your pussy don't make me none. Just don't start thinking yo shit don't stank just because you sucking the boss's dick."

Alaska was pissed as Sophia walked out of the room with her crew in tow. After that last remark Alaska wanted to jump up and slap fire to Sophia's ass but she didn't want to do it with no clothes on.

"What's wrong?" Santee' said as he woke up to see her angrily sitting there with her arms folded.

"Sophia and her little crew just walked in here and woke me up. She accused me of trying to fuck my way to the top and then she left."

"Did she now?" Santee' sat up and wrapped his arms around her waist. "Well I'm sorry she did that, but don't even trip. I'll be sure to check her about it later."

"Thanks, but that's okay. I don't want her thinking that I need you to fight my battles too. She just hating, which ain't nothing I haven't dealt with before so I think I can handle it."

"Very well then," Santee' replied kissing her neck.

"But speaking of help; how are things coming along with the search for Hank? Have any of your guys made any progress?"

"No," Santee' said as he stopped kissing her neck and pulled away from her. He leaned over his side of the bed and grabbed his underwear, putting them on underneath the sheet before standing up. "I'll be sure to check in with them for an update sometime later today though."

"Okay," Alaska replied noticing how quickly he pulled away from her. "Where are you going?" she asked as he put his pants back on.

"I have a meeting this morning, but I'll be back in a little while. You're welcome to stay here if you like."

"Thanks," Alaska said getting up, "but I have a few runs I need to make as well."

"Well then I'll call you later on tonight." Santee' said kissing her cheek and walking out of the room.

CHAPTER TWENTY NINE

Jay leaned on his cane as he climbed out of his truck and walked into the house he shared with Draya. It had been a few days since the shooting and although Jay wasn't laying his head there, he did go back to the house from time to time to get things that he needed. Today though, Jay's reason for going to the house was strictly to find out if there was any truth to what Vanessa had told him. Although Andraya wasn't there, Jay was searching the house for any clues he could find that might point to her betrayal. He looked through all the papers on her desk and logged into her email account to check her messages. He decided to go through all of her garbage cans too.

When Jay had just about given up his search, he came across a key that was taped to the bottom of the computer's keyboard. Looking around the room, Jay tugged on all the drawers to her desk until he came across one that was locked.

"Bingo," he said sticking the key inside. Jay wasn't sure exactly what he would find but he expected it to be more than just a manila folder filled with papers. Jay pulled the folder out and sat it on top of the desk before opening it and reading the first page. When he realized it was a life in-surance policy on his life in the amount of 3 million dollars, Jay instantly began to sweat as anger took over his body. If

Draya stood to get that much money upon his death, he had no choice but to believe what Vanessa told him was true.

Jay grabbed his phone from him pocket preparing to call Draya for the first time since he'd checked out. But before he could dial her number, her face appeared on the screen. Remaining as calm as he could, Jay answered.

"About time you called to check on me," he said as if nothing was wrong.

Andraya was surprised by his tone and she was happy he didn't answer the phone cussing her out.

"Yeah, sorry about that. I've been busy helping my mother get ready for her kidney transplant."

"Yeah okay," Jay said wondering why she would tell that lie when he knew she hadn't talked to her mother in years.

"No really," Draya explained. "With all that we've been going through I didn't get a chance to tell you that we've recently began speaking again. She needs a transplant so I got tested and found out I'm a match. The surgery will be next week." Draya lied.

Jay didn't know if he should believe her or not so he didn't say anything in reply.

"But enough about all that," Draya dismissed, "I called you because I miss my husband and I need to see you."

"Word," Jay finally replied. Now he definitely knew something was up. "Well why you don't meet me at the house. I'm not that far away so I could meet you there in twenty minutes."

"I'll see you then."

Draya disconnected the call and Jay shook his head. He couldn't believe his wife had flipped on him for money when he had given her everything she ever wanted and then some. "Bitches are never satisfied," Jay said as he went and prepared for Draya's arrival.

Fifteen minutes later, Jay sat inside his truck pretending he hadn't been inside the house yet when Andraya pulled up.

"Hey daddy!" she cooed as she jumped out of her car and ran over to him wrapping her arms around his neck. She began to kiss his lips and Jay had to fight the urge to push her away.

"C'mon, let's go in the house," Jay said finally pulling away. "You know how nosey Mrs. Bradley's ass is."

"Ain't that the truth," Andraya chuckled as she followed Jay inside.

As soon as he shut the door, Draya was all over him like flies on shit. Not knowing what her plan was, he cautiously went along with the flow, keeping his guard up at all times.

"I've missed you so much," Draya said between kisses. "I was going crazy when I heard about the shooting. I thought you were dead."

Is that why you started fucking the next nigga? Jay wanted to ask, but he wasn't ready to reveal his cards just yet. Instead he just sat back and let her do her thing as she began remove her clothes and his too. Dropping down to her knees, Draya began to suck him off as he kept one eye open surveying the scene. Although he was down to get a shot of his wife pussy one last time, Jay was aware of how bitches moved. They always thought they could catch a nigga slipping by blinding him with sex. But after an hour and two nuts went by, Jay realized Draya must've had something else up her sleeve.

After they had sex a few more times, Draya went to the kitchen to make some tacos leaving Jay wondering if he'd been wrong. Other than sending a few text messages, Draya hadn't done anything strange or out of the ordinary since she'd been there. The smell of the tacos made Jay get up and he followed the aroma until he was in the kitchen. Leaning against the doorframe, he watched Draya as she moved effortlessly around the kitchen and for a moment, he found himself missing their old life together. Even though Jay had a problem keeping his dick in his pants, Andraya had been the only girl he truly ever loved.

"Smells good," he said as he limped over to the stove and stole a spoonful of ground beef. Draya was an excellent cook and it had been a long time since Jay had a home cooked meal. He was excited to throw down, even if it was just tacos.

"Beat it," Draya said as she took the spoon from him and playfully smacked his hand. "Everything should be done in a minute. Have a seat in the den and I'll bring your plate out to you."

"Cool," Jay said grabbing a jalapeño from the bowl and popping it into his mouth.

As he sat down in front of the TV, Jay started to feel guilty for believing that Andraya was going to betray him. Although he still found the life insurance policy a little suspect, he didn't see any other signs that pointed to her guilt. Jay decided he would just fall back for now, and he reached for the remote, changing the channel to Sport Center. Just as Skip Bayless began to go into another hater fueled rant about LeBron James, Draya's cell phone started buzzing across the table. Jay hadn't even realized it was sitting there and he quickly picked it up once he did. Pressing the home button, Jay realized a text had just come through but he couldn't read it because her phone was locked.

Taking a swipe at her code, Jay entered her birthday and screen turned red notifying him that that was the incorrect passcode. Trying one more time, he entered their wedding date and just like that, the screen popped open. Tapping the little green box that said messages, Jay read the one that had just come through.

How much longer?

The text read. The contact didn't have a name and only a phone number was displayed at the top. Jay strolled through the text history and he soon found that the message had indeed come from that nigga Xavier. Pretending to be Draya, he texted back,

I'm almost ready. Where are u?

I'm in position at the front of the house. Just give me the word when it's time and I'll be ready.

Okay.

Jay read their text history over the last few days and he learned that their plan was to get him to let his guard down, and then when Draya give him the signal, Xavier would began beating on the door like he was the police. Thinking that Jay wouldn't go to the door strapped if he thought 5-0 was standing outside, Xavier would then ambush Jay, opening fire on him and killing him on the spot.

Jay quickly put the phone down when he heard Draya's footsteps as she finally made her way into the den.

"Here you go," She said placing the food down in front of him. Jay had been starving ten minutes ago, but now the food was the last thing on his mind. Draya went back to the kitchen to get their drinks and Jay knew he had to think fast. Now that he knew for sure what Draya's plan was, he could no longer delay the inevitable.

When Draya came back into the room, Jay stopped her before she was able to sit down and get comfortable.

"Damn babe, my phone is dead. Would you mind running upstairs to get my charger for me?" Jay asked.

"Sure baby, I'll be right back."

As soon as her feet hit the stairs, Jay grabbed her cell phone from the table and entered the passcode.

Get in place. Everything's ready. When you see the door open up ... blast him.

Jay hit the send button and he tapped his foot impatiently on the floor as he waited for confirmation. Just as Draya descended the last step, the little grey bubble turned into words.

I'm ready.

HEAVY

Jay was able to put the phone back in its place just as Draya rounded the corner.

"Baby I can't find your charger. You sure you left it upstairs?"

"You know what, I must have left it in the car," Jay smiled as she fell perfectly into his trap. "Do you mind running out there?"

"Sure," Draya sighed. She was ready to eat her food but she was trying to be nice, since she knew Jay only had a few hours left to live.

"Wait!" Jay called out right before her hand touched the knob. "Come and give me a kiss before you go."

"Boy!" Draya laughed out loud at his request. "You're so silly."

As she walked over, Jay took in the sight of her one last time. When they kissed, Draya got a weird surge throughout her body and she pulled away, looking at him strangely.

"I'll be right back," she said as she turned away and headed to the door.

The moment it creaked open, Jay heard the sound of gunfire erupting followed by her screams.

CHAPTER THIRTY

Santee's mansion was buzzing with activity as a crew of more than a hundred workers milled about the grounds. Watching from his bedroom terrace, Santee' and Alaska enjoyed a light breakfast as he kept a close eye on the entertainment company he'd hired for tonight's festivities. He wanted to make sure they were earning every cent of their fifteen thousand dollar fee and that none of the men were just sitting around twiddling their thumbs on his dime. As he glanced over the railing, he was pleased when he saw the men break off into smaller groups and begin working simultaneously to assemble the party's massive setup. From the seating arrangements to the one thousand square foot glass dance floor that would cover his swimming pool, there was a lot that needed to be done. One of the groups tackled the setup of the tables and chairs while another began assembly on the dance floor. A third group worked to erect the huge air conditioned tent that would house all the food, as well as, the full open bar.

"You really go all out for these parties, huh?" Alaska took a bite of her bacon as she watched the organized chaos below.

"Of course ma, that's why they're so legendary. It's a celebration of our success and prosperity. Some of the dope game's best and brightest travel from all over the country just to be in attendance. I can't very well have them go through all that trouble just to experience the ordinary now can I?"

"Well, I guess not," Alaska chuckled. She finished her breakfast as she watched the sun rise over the Vegas skyline. She couldn't help but think of Omar as she stared up at the heavens above. She wondered if he knew how much she missed him and if he was angry at her for her relationship with Santee'. Although Alaska knew he'd want her to be happy, she wasn't sure how he would feel about her doing so with a man he once called a friend.

As if he was reading her mind, Santee reached over and gently touched her hand. "I bet he's smiling down on you right now," he said softly.

"You think so?" Alaska replied, still looking to the sky.

"I guarantee it. When a man leaves this earth with love in his heart for a woman, that love becomes eternal. There's not a thing you could say or a decision you could make that would change that now. He knows that you're happy and that you're safe. That's all that matters."

"Thank you," Alaska said finally making eye contact with Santee'. His words warmed her heart and she was grateful for them. A lesser man would have faulted her for thinking of another man in his presence, but Santee' understood she was still grieving and that he couldn't rush the process.

Santee' lifted her hand into the air beckoning her to come over to him. He held on to it softly as she walked around the small patio table that separated them. With the sun shining down and casting a silhouette behind her, Santee' admired how beautiful she was in this moment. Still seated, he placed his hands upon her hips and gazed up into her eyes before he spoke.

"There's no need to thank me, ma. Just promise me that you'll continue to let me be the one who makes you happy."

"I promise," Alaska whispered as she lovingly cupped the sides of his face with her hands.

His favorite part of her anatomy was directly in front of his face and Santee' couldn't help himself as he loosened the tie that held her silk robe together exposing her completely naked body. The warm morning air tickled her nipples as it breezed across her chest. She felt Santee's fingertips on her skin as his hands ran up the back of her legs until they reached her ass. Firmly gripping her cheeks, he massaged them as he began a trail of wet kisses starting at her navel. She kept her pussy completely shaven and Santee' could see her clit as it jumped in anticipation of his touch. Alaska lifted her right leg and placed her foot on the armrest of his chair so that she could give him full access to what had now become his favorite snack. When the wetness and heat from Santee's tongue finally made contact with her clit, Alaska let the robe fall below her shoulders and her head fell back as she totally forgot about the workers below them.

She struggled to stand as Santee' alternated between sucking on her clit and fucking her with his tongue. His head game was intoxicating and Alaska had to fight the urge to scream out his name. She placed her hands behind his head so she could steady herself as she began to slowly grind her hips into his face. He quickly synced with her rhythm, flicking his tongue across her clit with each thrust she made. When he knew she was about to cum, Santee' placed his mouth directly over her clit and stuck two of his fingers deep inside her pussy. Unable to hold back any longer, a deep moan escaped her lips as she passionately called out his name. Santee' smiled in satisfaction when a moment later her juices exploded all over his hands and face.

"Damn papi, that shit was amazing." Alaska removed her foot from the chair as she used the table to steady herself. She was spent and her legs felt like jello but she couldn't leave without at least returning the favor. Grabbing his hand, she led him back inside. It would be another two hours before the two of them finally came up for air.

HEAVY

Alaska wiggled her body as she tried to free herself from the comfort of Santee's strong arms without waking him up. She sat up and had almost successfully climbed out of the bed when Santee' playfully reached out and pulled her back down again.

"Where do you think you're going?" He placed his face in the crock of her neck and began nibbling on her earlobe.

"I have to go get ready for the party," Alaska moaned, enjoying the feeling of his warm breath against her skin. "If I don't leave now, I'll never make it back here in time."

"A woman as beautiful as you should always make her grand entrance by arriving fashionably late anyway."

"Flattery will get you everywhere Mr. Santee'." Alaska smiled seductively as she leaned over and kissed his lips. Her right hand rubbed his manhood and she could feel it begin to grow underneath the one thousand thread count sheets. When she knew he was totally distracted by her touch, Alaska released him and jumped out of the bed, giggling as she ran away towards his master bathroom. But the joke was on her when she realized Santee' was on her heels before she could even make it across the room.

"Gotcha," he said as he wrapped his arms around her and the two of them fell to the floor in laughter. Alaska couldn't remember the last time she felt this good. Santee' was slowly breaking down the walls around her heart and she had to admit, it felt damn good.

Using his chest as leverage, Alaska separated her body from his and stood up. "I'm going to take a shower," she said seductively looking over her shoulder, "Feel free to join me."

The love birds somehow managed to keep their hands off each other as they showered together and then got dressed. Santee' walked her to the door and she kissed him goodbye before she jumped into her brand new Audi A7 and drove away.

Alaska exited Santee's upscale neighborhood in Green Valley and merged onto I-215 West heading back towards Las Vegas. As she weaved the luxury vehicle smoothly in and out of traffic, she removed her phone from her purse and used the voice activation feature to call Jackie. She was more than an hour late for her appointment but she needed to let Jackie know she was still coming.

"Hey Ms. Thang," Jackie answered her call on the first ring. "I was wondering when you were gonna call and let me know you found somebody else to do your hair for the party. 'Cause surely you don't think Ms. Jackie will be running her magic fingers through that mane of yours when you're more than an hour late for your scheduled appointment."

"Aww... c'mon Jac, don't be like that boo. You know I love you, girl." Alaska laughed as she switched lanes and jumped on I-15.

Jackie had been doing her hair since she moved to Vegas, and Alaska loved her to death.

"Mm hmm. And what's love got to do with it?" Jackie asked, smacking her lips.

"Apparently a lot," Alaska smiled, thinking of Santee', "but I'll tell you all about that when I get there."

"Alright now, honey! Ms. Alaska's got some tea to spill." Jackie perked up at the mention of her favorite pastime; other people's business. "Let me go so I can fill up my tea pot and get my tea cups ready. I'll see you when you get her girl."

Alaska shook her head and laughed at her friend. "Alright love, I'll see you in a minute," she said before disconnecting the call.

She thought about calling Sophia next but decided against it. Since their run in at Santee's house the other day, Alaska hadn't heard from her despite leaving several messages on her voicemail. Sophia made it seem as if she could care less about Alaska's budding relationship with Santee', but her sudden cold shoulder made Alaska wonder if that was really true. She even asked Santee' outright if anything had ever went down between the two of them, but he vehemently denied that it had, leaving Alaska to feel a little like she was missing pieces to a puzzle. Alaska had never been one to just sit back and play the fool though, so she vowed to keep an eye on the situation. If too many red flags appeared, she would have no problem calling an audible on their relationship. Alaska knew she would see Sophia tonight at the party. If she truly had an issue with her, Alaska hoped she would finally be a woman and speak on it. Otherwise, Alaska planned to keep it moving with no love lost. If there was one thing she knew for sure, it was that she was never pressed about having a friendship with the next bitch.

Alaska made it to Jackie's salon in record time. As she pulled into the parking lot, she spotted an empty space right in front of the entrance and she quickly whipped her car into it. She thanked God that she didn't have to walk more than five steps in this ridiculous one hundred and ten degree heat as she grabbed her Berkin bag and got out of the car. It was a Saturday afternoon in the summer and the salon was in full turn up mode. Each of the seven stylists had multiple clients waiting to be serviced; including Jackie. But Alaska didn't have to wait. Jackie called her over the moment she walked through the door and Alaska happily sashayed pass the long line of side eyes and smacking lips.

"Uh-uh," a cute dark skinned girl with hair down to her butt stood up and called Jackie out. "How you just gone let her walk right in and get in the chair? I had an appointment and I've been waiting here for more than an hour."

"And if you wanna keep that appointment, I suggest you keep your little outburst to a minimum. I run this salon and I adjust *my* schedule the way I see fit. If you don't like that Ms. Thang, feel free to go ahead and exit stage left." Jackie's tone was unapologetic. She didn't even wait to see which option the girl would choose before she turned around and followed Alaska back into the area that housed her private station.

"The nerve of some bitches," Jackie said as she rolled her eyes and shut the door.

"Girl, you are so wrong," Alaska chuckled as she sat down in the chair. "I kind of feel bad for the girl now."

"You wanna switch places wit her then?"

"Girl bye," Alaska said waving her hand dismissively. "I said I *kind of* felt bad for her. That don't mean I'm about to pull out my checkbook and start donating to charity."

"And there you have it," Jackie said grabbing her smock and tying it around her waist.

The two women fell out laughing as Jackie got started on Alaska's hair, removing the rubber band that held together her messy ponytail. For the next two hours, Jackie worked her magic while the pair caught up and talked about everything under the sun. Alaska spilled the tea on everything that had been going on in her life since Omar died. The only details she left out were that of her newfound profession. It wasn't that she didn't trust Jackie, but Alaska understood that whenever possible, it was always better to leave the ones you love clueless about your dealings in the streets. The less they knew the better off they'd be.

Jackie grabbed a can of Mizani oil sheen from her station and lightly sprayed a layer onto Alaska's hair. Once she was done with the finishing touches, she spun the chair all the way around until Alaska was facing the mirror.

"Voila!"

When Alaska's reflection appeared in the mirror, the sleek and sweeping up-do Jackie created made her jaw drop.

"Bitch, you need to insure them hands with Lloyd's of London 'cause I promise you they have been anointed by God himself."

Jackie removed the cape from around her neck and Alaska stood up to get a better look at her hair in the mirror.

"Well, thank you Ms. Alaska honey. You know she does what she can," Jackie said, referring to herself in the third person.

"Yes, well, *she* definitely did that honey," Alaska smiled as she handed Jackie a check for two hundred dollars. It was twice her normal fee but Alaska always tipped her friend well. She worked miracles every time she touched her head so for Alaska, it was worth every penny. And as far as she was concerned, Jackie should've been charging more than a hundred dollars for her services anyway.

Alaska grabbed her purse and the ladies said goodbye with hugs and air kisses.

"Do me a favor and send Ms. *I Had An Appointment* back here on your way out, would you?" Jackie rolled her eyes to the sky and Alaska fall out laughing.

"I sure will," she said as she walked out the door.

The amount of customers in the waiting room had doubled since Alaska's arrival, but she wasn't at all surprised to find the young girl still sitting in the same spot with a sour look on her face.

"Your turn," Alaska smirked as they made eye contact. She heard the girl call her a bitch under her breath as she passed by and Alaska just smiled. There was no point in getting upset about the truth.

Alaska *was* a bitch. And she felt like the head one in charge as she peeled out of the parking lot and headed home to get ready for the party.

CHAPTER THIRTY ONE

Santee'

Santee' sipped on a glass of yak as he admired the hundreds of party goers who were dressed in all white and littered throughout his 2,000 square feet back yard. Hustlers from each coast mingled about peacefully as some of them closed six figure deals over steak, lobster and expensive cognacs. It was an image that made Santee' swell with pride. The people surrounding him at this moment represented his second family. They were the best and the brightest of his team and each one of them had helped to take the organization from its humble beginnings to the national syndicate it was today. They were a diverse group of men and women but they all spoke the same universal language; loyalty above all else. In the twenty plus years since Santee' started this organization, he never once had to deal with the issue of treachery within his own team. He made sure everybody ate well and he always remained fair whenever any issues did arise.

As Santee' scanned the crowd, he searched for the one face he had been waiting to see all night long. Alaska Drake had quickly become an important part of his life, and he wasn't afraid to admit to himself that he had fallen in love with her. In his mind's eye everything about her was perfect. From the way she walked to the way she talked and everything else in between, Santee' hadn't been this smitten by a woman in a long time. Checking his watch, Santee' decided to give her a call to make sure everything was okay. As he pulled his phone out of his pocket, he stopped when he felt a hand touch his shoulder.

"Hey," whisper the familiar voice from behind.

Santee' turned to see Alaska standing there looking more beautiful than ever and for a moment he was speechless.

"Hey yourself," he finally replied after finding his words again. "My God, you look absolutely gorgeous."

"Why thank you sir," Alaska smiled as she did a little twirl allowing him to get a full look at her body in the skin tight dress. She looked like an angel all dressed in white and Santee' nodded with approval before leaning in and kissing her cheek.

"I was starting to think you weren't coming," Santee' said still holding her hand.

"Fashionably late, remember?" Alaska smiled as she stopped a waiter carrying a tray of champagne. She graciously grabbed herself a glass. "Everything looks amazing. You really know how to throw a party baby."

Santee' smiled at the compliment and took her hand once again, "Come with me. I know you just got here, but I have a few people I would like for you to meet."

"One sec," Alaska said as she put the champagne flute to her mouth and tossed it back. "Okay, I'm ready," she smiled as she sat the glass down on a nearby table.

The first gentleman Santee' introduced her to was his accountant, Kahlil Ackerman. Kahlil was a forty-something chocolate skin brother from the Washington D.C. area, who looked more like a personal trainer then he did a lawyer. Alaska admired his muscular arms as she smiled and shook his hand, "Hello, it's very nice to meet you."

"Likewise," Kahlil replied. The three of them exchanged small talk for a few more minutes before Santee' moved on to the next guest. They did this until Alaska met the entire top tier of the organization. From his lawyers to his lieutenants, Santee' wanted her to meet all of them so that if anything should ever happen to him, she would know just who to call. After they were finished, Alaska excused herself to go to the ladies room. She couldn't wait to run into Sophia tonight and she scanned the crowd looking for her. But the sea of people dressed in all white made it impossible for her to spot any one person.

Giving up her search for now, Alaska went inside the bathroom and handled her business. When she was done, she returned to the party to find Santee' standing on the stage with a microphone in his hand. He spotted her and waved for her to come over and stand next to him.

"Good evening everybody, can I have your attention please?" Santee's voice came over the speakers and everyone quickly gave him their undivided attention.

"Thank you. I would like to take the time out to thank each and every one of you for coming out tonight. I know some of you took flights or drove long hours to get here, and I truly appreciate that." Santee' paused as his guest clapped in acknowledgement. "Tonight is a celebration," he continued, "It's a celebration of success, love, and most of all family. If you are standing here tonight it means that I consider you apart of my family and your presence within this organization is invaluable. So, with that being said, I would like to propose a toast." Santee' lifted his glass in the air, Alaska and the rest of the crowd did the same.

"To a lifetime of continued success, love and loyalty; Salute."

"Salute!" The crowd responded in unison while clinking together their glasses.

"I have a surprise for you," Santee' whispered in Alaska's ear. He took to the microphone once again while he still had everyone's attention.

HEAVY

"One last thing," he said, holding up his finger to the audience. "Another reason I wanted you all here tonight was to help me celebrate a very special moment. For those of you who don't know, this beautiful lady standing to my left is Ms. Alaska Drake. Even though she has only recently come into my life, she still managed to find a way to steal my heart."

The entire backyard let out a collective awe, and Alaska stood there in shock as Santee' turned to her and got down on one knee.

"Oh my God! Are you serious?" Alaska's mouth was gaping open and she instinctively covered it with her hands. She couldn't believe this was happening right now. She hadn't even come to terms with the guilt she felt for dating him, and yet here he was about to ask her to marry him. A part of her was flattered that she'd made that much of an impression on him that he'd want to spend the rest of his life with her, but another part of her was upset with him for not at least asking her how she felt about it first. Alaska found it very inconsiderate of him not to ask her if she ever even wanted to get married again.

Santee' looked up at Alaska with excited eyes. He reached into his jacket pocket and pulled out a small square ring box. The iconic light blue coloring let everybody know the ring inside was from Tiffany's. Santee' opened the box and revealed a stunning, seven karat princess cut diamond ring. It sparkled brighter than the stars in the sky above as he held it up for Alaska to see.

"I cherish the day you walked into my life and I never want you to leave. Please allow me the honor of taking care of you and waking up to your beautiful face every single day. Alaska Drake, I love you. Will you marry me?"

Alaska felt like a deer caught in headlights as Santee' and the rest of the guest waited for her response. Her heart and her mind were both telling her to run, but Alaska just couldn't bring herself to break his heart in front of all these people. Instead, she let the word *yes* slip from her lips and everybody went wild. Santee' slipped the ring on her finger and scooped her up into his arms, spinning her around as he kissed her. All of a sudden there was a sea of smiling faces clapping and offering their congratulations, but Alaska instinctively honed in on the one face in the crowd that wasn't.

Sophia.

If looks could kill, everybody in her direct line of vision would have been pushing up daises right now, including Alaska and Santee'.

"What the fuck is her problem," Alaska asked Santee'; through clinched teeth and a fake smile.

"What are you talking about?"

Alaska said nodding her head in the direction where Sophia had been standing.

"I don't see anyone," Santee' said, puzzled.

"It was Sophia. She was standing there looking at me like she wanted to take me out the game."

"What?" Santee' frowned, "C'mon, baby. We just got engaged. Don't ruin it with all that crazy talk. Maybe you just misread her expression."

Alaska was livid. "Don't do that shit," she said finally dropping the fake smile from her face.

"Don't do what?" Santee' asked taken aback by her attitude. "And who are you cursing at?"

"Don't dismiss me and tell me I didn't see what I know I saw. If the two of you are still fucking, then you can go ahead and take this ring back right now 'cause I'm telling you I don't have time for the foolishness and fuckery."

"Listen," Santee' said sternly. "For the last time, Sophia and I have never had a sexual relationship and we never will. I told you once before, I'm not a liar. But if you don't believe me then maybe you should give me the ring back. Otherwise, I need you to calm down. Now wait right here while I go try to find her and figure out what's wrong."

Exasperated, Alaska threw her hands up in the air and before quickly letting them fall back to her side.

"Whatever," she said as she walked away from Santee' and headed over to the bar. As she waited for the bartender to bring her a double shot of patron, Alaska stared at the flawless diamond that now sat on her left ring finger. She had to admit it was gorgeous, but she still had half a mind to take it off and leave it right there on the bar before she turned around and walked out the door. The bartender sat her drink down in front of her and Alaska quickly picked it up. She tossed her head back and let the burning liquid slide down her throat. Slamming the shot glass back down on the bar, she told him to give her another one just as she heard someone calling her name from behind. She turned around to see two of the other housewives, Kim and Daphne, standing behind her.

"Hey girl, congratulations," Kim smiled and reached out to give Alaska a hug. Daphne followed suit. Alaska hadn't seen either of them since they caught her in bed with Santee'.

"Thank you," Alaska said as she and Daphne pulled apart from their quick embrace.

"Sorry about the other day," Daphne apologized. "Sophia can be a real bitch sometimes but she means well."

"It's cool." Alaska said waving it off. She was embarrassed enough as it was. She didn't need to keep talking about it.

"So I can't believe somebody got ole' Sebastian to finally settle down," Kim teased.

"I know right. We gotta take a shot to celebrate this moment." Daphne held up two fingers signaling the bartender to bring more shots.

"Well I'm glad somebody's happy for me," Alaska said as she rolled her eyes.

"What do you mean? Everybody seems pretty excited to me." Kim said, confused.

"Not Sophia's hatin' ass. She stood in the corner shooting daggers at me right after Santee' proposed."

Daphne and Kim glanced at each other.

"Well, you know how spoiled little girls can be," Daphne said shrugging her shoulders.

Alaska was about to ask her what she meant by that, but she was interrupted when the bartender arrived with their shots.

"To love, marriage and a baby carriage," Daphne sang as the women laughed and clanked their glasses together.

"Cheers!"

Alaska chatted with the women a little while longer, and then she said her goodbye's and went off in search of Santee'. She wanted to let him know she was leaving. Being that they just got engaged, she knew he would probably want to spend the night together, but Alaska needed a little bit more time to actually think about her decision. She simply didn't trust Santee' enough yet, and the fact that he had been gone looking for Sophia so long only further added to her suspicions. Alaska walked around the entire first floor of the massive home. She searched the living room, kitchen and den area looking for Santee'. With no luck on the first floor, she ascended the stairs to the second. She checked all four bedrooms, including Santee's bedroom, the computer and game rooms down the hall but all of them were empty.

What the fuck?

Alaska stood in the hallway getting more pissed off by the second. If Santee' and Sophia were truly fucking around behind her back, she would make sure there was hell to pay for both of them muthafuckas. Alaska was about to head back downstairs to see if somehow she'd overlooked them, when she heard the sound of voices coming from the other end of the hall.

"His study!" Alaska said remembering the lavish room with cherry wood paneling and expensive furniture.

She had only been in there once before when she came over to talk to Santee' about something a few weeks ago and she'd forgotten it was there. Her heart began racing as she crept down the hallway, careful not to make too much noise. As she got closer, Sophia and Santee's voices became clearer and Alaska unconsciously held her breath as she listened in.

"I told you that you shouldn't have made her a part of this team in the first place." Sophia spat angrily, "Now you're sitting here telling me you 'bout to marry this bitch. I know the pussy can't be that damn good."

"Watch your fucking mouth," Santee' responded shooting her a warning look. "And I don't give a fuck *what* you said. This is my organization and I make changes around here whenever the hell I see fit. The only choice you have in the matter is to simply deal with it."

Sophia rolled her eyes and tightly folded her arms across her chest. She was furious. So much so that if she didn't believe the situation would end fatally on her part, she probably would have jumped across the table and attached Santee'.

"I just need you to explain to me how you're ready to marry someone you've only known for six fuckin' months. Who the hell does that?"

Santee' had enough. He was trying to be understanding with Sophia but now she'd pushed him too far with her smart ass mouth.

"Understand this," Santee' stood up and walked from behind his desk until the two of them were face to face, "I don't *have* to explain a muthafuckin thing to you. But since you asked, go ahead and have a seat 'cause I'm about to do it anyway. Omar was a good man and he and I were about to make a lot of money together until your triflin' whorish ass fucked that up."

Alaska's heart dropped at the mention of Omar's name. She knew something wasn't right with Sophia lately, but she never would have guessed her issues had anything to do with

Omar. She needed more details so she inched her body even closer to the door, making sure she could hear every word as Santee' continued.

"You knew that man was in love with his wife. Once you returned from Colombia he was hardly checking for you, yet you relentlessly pursued him anyway. *Then*, when he wouldn't give you what you wanted, in true crazy bitch fashion, you paid your crack-head brother to *kill* him, instead of just walking away and taking the L like a real woman. Now you expect me to suffer and deny the feelings I have for Alaska just because you've become a pawn in your own fuckin' game?" Santee' asked incredulously. "Well, I'm sorry baby girl, but I refuse to do it. And furthermore, this will be the last time I ever speak on this matter with you, so I suggest you build a bridge and get over it. 'Cause at the end of the day, no matter how you or anybody else really feels about it, Alaska isn't going anywhere anytime soon."

Sophia didn't say a word, but the look on her face as she stared him down spoke volumes. Santee' recognized it as a look of pure contempt, and one he never in a million years would have thought he'd see come across her face when she looked at him, but still he refused to give in.

"And by the way," he added, matching the intensity of her gaze. "If you even *think* about harming one hair on her pretty little head, I will personally hunt you down and kill you myself."

His words cut Sophia deeply and she had to fight hard to hold back the tears that were threatening to spill from her eyes. With nothing left to say, Sophia offered Santee' her back as she spun around on her six inch heels and stormed away.

Outside the door, Alaska's eyes filled with tears and her heart crumbled to the floor as she replayed Santee's words. *"All this time he knew,"* she whispered. The realization that she had been sleeping with the enemy sunk in, and she felt like an even bigger fool than the two of them had already played her for.

"You muthafuckas are going to pay," Alaska declared as she back pedaled away from the door and back down the hallway. "I promise you that."

CHAPTER THIRTY TWO

Sophia

The tires on Sophia's Range Rover screeched loudly as she threw the SUV in reverse and backed out of Santee's driveway. She was so upset after her conversation with him, that she didn't even bother telling her date that she was leaving.

He'll figure it out, Sophia thought as she put on her seatbelt and guided her truck in the direction of I-215. She was on her way to the weed spot to grab another loud pack before she headed home. Sophia smoked weed like a chimney and the urge only worsened when she was angry.

"Ugh! I can't believe this muthafucka proposed to her," she spat, reaching in the ashtray to retrieve the blunt she'd left in there earlier. It was the only thing that could calm her down in this moment as she welcomed the burn of the smoke as it hit the back of her throat. She only copped the good shit, so after a few hits of the potent drug, the THC made its way inside her bloodstream and quickly mellowed her out. Sophia put the burning blunt back in the ashtray and continued down 215. Her mind was in overdrive as she tried to figure out a way to stop Santee' and Alaska's wedding from ever taking place.

Regret washed over Sophia as she exited the highway and took the shortcut to the weed spot. Hindsight was 20/20 and now that some time had passed, Sophia realized she should have just forgiven Omar and got rid of Alaska instead. After all, she was the real threat to her relationship with Omar. If Sophia had just eliminated Alaska from the picture, Omar would have been able to see that they were truly meant to be together. Sadly, there would never be a chance for them now. But what was even worse was that Alaska was still around to serve as a constant reminder that she was everything Sophia wasn't. And that was precisely why Sophia couldn't allow her to marry Santee'. She'd already lost to her once, but she'd be damned if she ever let Alaska beat her again.

Sophia finally arrived at the Marble Manor projects and she parked her truck alongside the curb outside of Shorty's unit.

"What's good Ms. Lady?" Shorty stood to greet her as she walked across the large dirt patch that served as his lawn.

"Hey Shorty," she returned as she made her way onto the porch. "I hope you got some fire for me today, 'cause a bitch nerves is all the way bad right about now."

"Awe shit," Shorty chuckled, holding open the screen door for her as they went into the house. "Who done fucked up and pissed you off?"

"Long story," Sophia said waving her hand dismissively. Shorty was a drug dealer, not a therapist. Therefore, Sophia opted to skip the small talk and instead she quickly got what she came for before saying her goodbyes and heading home.

It was only a short drive from Shorty's house to her condo, which was located on the Las Vegas strip. She stopped at the store to grab some blunts and two bottles of wine. Once she was home, Sophia wasted no time removing the six inch Jimmy Choo sandals that had been torturing her feet all night long. She tossed her purse onto the kitchen countertop and then she unzipped the skin tight bandage dress she picked out specifically for tonight's party and she let it fall to the floor. The dress was so snug she chose not to wear any underwear underneath it, leaving her butt naked as she stood in the middle of her kitchen floor. The drapes were still open on the condo's floor to ceiling windows that overlooked the Las Vegas Strip, but Sophia could care less as she walked across the room to retrieve a wine glass. She popped the cork on the wine bottle and poured herself a full glass of the dark red liquid. Just as she was about to take the first sip, Sophia heard a noise coming from her bedroom and she froze.

She could hear the sound of someone ruffling through her things and she grabbed the .22 out of her purse and began to slowly walk down the hallway leading to her bedroom. The noise got louder the closer she got, but it stopped by the time she reached the door. The door was slightly ajar and Sophia could see the light from her nightstand peeking through the cracks. She held her breath as she listened for more movement. Suddenly, the door began to open wider as she felt something brush up against her leg.

"What the …," Sophia looked down to find Cornbread, her brother's cat, purring as it rubbed against her leg. She forgot the cat was even there and she figured the poor thing was probably searching for food since she hadn't remembered to leave any out. "Awe, come 'ere," she said as she bent down and scooped the cat into her arms. "Your little sneaky ass was about to get blown away." she chuckled.

Sophia stroked Cornbread's soft golden brown fur as she went into her room in search of something to wear. She threw on a t-shirt and a pair of boy shorts, and headed back to the kitchen to finish her glass of wine. As she rounded the corner, Sophia didn't even notice the figure that was now sitting at her kitchen table until she was a few steps in front of it.

"What the fuck!" Sophia spat as the figure came into view. "How the hell did you get in my house?"

"Now Sophia, is that any way to greet a friend?" Alaska smirked as she stood up from the table. "I thought you would be happy to see me. You left the party so early we didn't even get a chance to celebrate my engagement together."

Sophia just stared at her like she was crazy. She didn't want to mistakenly say anything that would set Alaska off so she remained quiet. She wasn't sure what her problem was, but Sophia deduced it was much deeper than her not sticking around to celebrate their engagement, from the gun Alaska held at her side.

"So ..." Alaska said removing two bottles from a paper bag as she continued, "I took the liberty of bringing the celebration here to you."

Sophia recognized the bell shaped Patrón bottle immediately, but she was unsure as to the contents of the glass vial filled with a clear liquid sitting next to it. Cornbread jumped out of her arms as Alaska lifted the gun in Sophia's direction as she walked over to the wet bar. She kept the barrel trained on Sophia's forehead as she grabbed a shot glass then made her way back to where Sophia was standing.

"Have a seat," Alaska demanded, pointing the gun in her face. Sophia was livid that Alaska had the audacity to pull a gun on her in her own home, but still she did as she was told. She'd left her strap back in the bedroom, so she knew it wouldn't be wise for her to pop off like she really wanted to.

"We're going to play a little game," Alaska informed her as she circled the table like a vulture circling its prey. "The rules are fairly simple; I ask you a question, you tell me the answer. If for some reason I ask you a question and you decide to lie to me, then you'll be enjoying one of these here cyanide laced Patrón shots."

Sophia watched as Alaska used a needle to extract the cyanide from the vial. She then filled the shot glass with tequila, followed by two drops of the deadly liquid. Sophia wasn't sure how much was needed to kill someone, but she knew even the smallest amount could take out a grown man twice her size.

"What is this about?" Sophia asked in the calmest voice she could muster. She was reaching her boiling point, but she knew she had to remain calm as long as Alaska had a gun and she didn't.

"I'm asking the fuckin' questions here!" Alaska said slamming her fist against the table.

Sophia nodded her head and raised her hands in surrender, "Okay, fine."

"First question," Alaska said sliding the shot glass in front of Sophia. "Why did you kill my husband?" Alaska had already heard part of the story but she needed to know more.

"What are you talking about?" Sophia stared at Alaska and ginned. She wasn't sure how Alaska found out, but she enjoyed the fact that Alaska now knew who was really responsible for her pain. "I thought you already knew the identity of your husband's killer? What in the world would make you think I had anything to do with it?" She asked playing innocent.

Alaska didn't have time to play games, and she pushed the shot glass even closer as she leaned over Sophia's shoulder and spoke directly in her ear.

"Do you have any idea what cyanide does to your body once it enters your system, Sophia?" Alaska stood up straight and walked around to the front of the chair. She squatted down so that she was eye level with Sophia before she continued. "Within just a few seconds, your blood cells will rapidly start to lose oxygen as it becomes increasingly difficult for you to breathe. While you're struggling to fight for each breath you take, your heart will begin to give out and it will soon go into full cardiac arrest. The rest of your body my love, will then be inundated with multiple seizures as you suffocate and have a heart attack all at the *same damn time*. Sounds like an awful way to die doesn't it?"

Alaska grabbed the shot glass from the tabled and handed it to Sophia. "Now, I'm going to ask you one more time; why did you kill my fucking husband?"

"Fine," Sophia sighed as she took the glass from Alaska's hand and placed it back on the table. "You want the truth; I'll be more than happy to give it to you. But you have to promise me something first."

"How about I promise not to blow your fuckin' brains out?" Alaska replied incredulously. Sophia knew it was risky to throw out demands when she wasn't the one holding the gun. But she also knew the next words out of her mouth could mean the difference between life and death for her.

"You're right," Sophia said with pleading eyes, "I'm not exactly in the position to be handing out request. But I promise I will tell you the truth and nothing but it, if you can promise me that you won't go through with this engagement to marry my father..."

"Wait ... what?" Alaska unconsciously lowered the gun as her brain tried to process the statement Sophia just made. "Santee' is your father?"

"99.9999 percent," Sophia smirked. She knew giving Alaska that information would make her think twice about taking her life. Nobody in their right mind would ever bring beef to her father's doorstep, and if Alaska decided to kill her tonight, she would be doing just that. Or at least that's what Sophia wanted her to think. As she waited for Alaska's response, Sophia wondered if her father would actually give a fuck if she was killed or not. The state of their relationship since Omar's death had been rocky to say the least, and Santee' even threatened to kill her himself if she did anything to hurt his precious Alaska. Sophia rolled her eyes at the thought.

"So what'll it be?" she asked as Alaska stood in front of her looking completely dumbfounded. Suddenly, Alaska snapped. She picked up the poison filled syringe and grabbed Sophia, putting her in a headlock.

"Bitch, I told you not to fucking lie to me," she spat. Spit formed at the sides of her mouth and sweat covered her brow. She put the tip of the syringe to Sophia's neck, pressing hard enough to break the skin, but not hard enough to inject its contents.

"WAIT!" Sophia yelled, pleading for Alaska not to push the needle into her skin any further. "I can prove it. Just look around you."

The condo's open floor plan allowed Alaska to see past the kitchen and into the living room. Her eyes darted back and forth as the various pictures on the wall slowly came into focus. There were snapshots of Sophia and Santee' throughout every phase of Sophia's life. From an olive-skinned little girl wearing pigtails and fancy dresses, to a young woman rocking expensive weaves and red bottoms; Santee' was right there in every picture.

A wave of nausea came over Alaska as she realized she had just agreed to marry the father of the woman who was responsible for her husband' death. While claiming to love her and also promising that he would help her clap back, Santee' knew all along that his daughter had been the one responsible. It was all too much for her to handle. But as Alaska stood there with the gun in her hand, she knew she had to make a decision.

"Okay," Alaska finally spoke. "I'll call off the engagement. Now tell me everything."

Alaska listened as Sophia dropped another bombshell informing her that Big Hank was her twin brother. Although Santee' had been a part of Sophia and her twin brother's lives since the day they were born, very few people knew that he had any children. Sophia and her brother were both born in her father's native country of Colombia. At the time, Santee' was embattled in a bloody war with the Italian's back in the States, and he sent his family into exile as a safety precaution when Sophia's mom was six months pregnant. Up until the age of five Sophia, her mother Michelle, and her brother Henry, or Hank for short, were officially citizens of the country of Colombia. Even after they returned to the

8

states, Santee' kept them sheltered and only revealed their relation when absolutely necessary.

When it was time to enroll the twins in school, he stripped them of their last name and replaced it with Smith. He even went as far as to have a school bus drop them off at a home registered to a Mr. and Mrs. Leroy Smith in an effort to throw any potential threats off their trail. Shortly after they were dropped off by the school bus, one of Santee's drivers would arrive to take them to their real home. This charade continued until the day they graduated from high school. Although Santee' believed he was doing what was best for his children, he didn't realize the true effects it had on them until much later, and after it was already too late. Not having their father's recognition in public and always being forced to pretend to be someone else, gave both Sophia and Hank a complex about who they really were and it forced them to seek praise and approval elsewhere in the streets. Hank eventually found his in the form of a crack and cocaine habit, while Sophia was still searching for hers in the arms of no good men.

She wanted desperately to be a kingpin's wife because she believed it would somehow finally prove her worth to her father. Despite telling everyone that she had been the original cocaine housewife, joining the team only after the unexpected death of her husband, Sophia had never actually been married. In fact, she'd never even been close to being anyone's wife. Her longest relationship lasted only five months, and it ended after she found out he was married too. Although she liked him a lot, Sophia had a complex about playing the background and he simply hadn't been "boss" enough to make her get over it. After that whole disaster, Sophia vowed that she was going to take a break and close her ever revolving door of men.

Then she met Omar.

Their meeting had happened strictly by chance, but in Sophia's eyes it was more like fate. The night they spent together in Colombia was like a fairytale, and when she returned to the states, Sophia thought for sure he was going to make her his girl. However, she didn't hear from him for two whole weeks. She was devastated and angry, refusing to believe the chemistry she felt for him hadn't been reciprocated. Sophia was convinced that Omar was her soul mate. She had absolutely no chill when it came to pursuing him, and eventually Omar got fed up with the situation.

When she started blowing up his phone with all kind of phone calls and text messages, he finally dropped the bomb. He proceeded to tell her that he was married, and had been for years. He informed her that he loved Alaska, while he was very fond of her, the two of them could never be together sexually again. Sophia had heard everything Omar said, but still his words never truly registered with her brain. While smoking a blunt with Hank a few days later, she told him about the situation and mused about how she would pay good money to have someone dead Omar for the way he played her. Sophia's comment had initially just been a joke. But Hank recognized the potential for a handsome payday if he could pull off the murder and a robbery at the same time. He soon convinced his sister that Omar's indiscretions against her had to be dealt with. He volunteered to be her hired gunman but before Sophia had time to really think it through, Hank was on the phone putting their murder plot into motion.

By the time Sophia finished running down her story, Alaska was completely distraught. She couldn't believe that everything she'd gone through in the last few months was a direct result of Omar's inability to keep his dick in his pants.

Sophia watched her closely as she slowly stood up from the table. Her expression was blank and Sophia had no idea what she was thinking.

"Thank you for telling me the truth," Alaska said as she began to place everything she brought with her back into the bag. She then took the cyanide filled shot glass and poured it out in to the kitchen sink behind her. "I'll be going now."

That's right. You better think twice bitch, Sophia laughed to herself.

"Listen, I'm really sorry about the way this all went down," she lied as she led Alaska to the door. She was so excited that she was finally able to use her "daughter of a kingpin" card, that Sophia didn't realize her fate until Alaska placed the gun to the back of her head.

"Yup… me too bitch," Alaska said as she smiled and pulled the trigger.

CHAPTER THIRTY THREE

Santee'

Santee' hadn't heard from Alaska since she walked out of the party last night without saying goodbye. He called her phone more than a dozen times, and he'd even sent her a few text messages, but he never got a response. Santee' knew he had sprung the engagement thing on her without any warning, so he figured she was just taking some time to really think things over. As he shuffled through the papers that were stacked on his desk, Santee' checked the time as he wondered why Sophia wasn't there yet. It was the last day of the month and she usually arrived bright and early to ride with him over to the warehouse so that they could perform their monthly audit. Picking up the phone, Santee' dialed her number.

Just like Alaska's, Sophia's phone went straight to voicemail without ever ringing.

"What the hell," Santee' said out loud as he hung up the phone. Something wasn't right and he needed to find out what it was.

"Ricky. I need to see you in my study for a minute," Santee' said to the head of his security detail by intercom.

"Sure thing, boss. I'll be up there in a minute."

As Santee' waited for his arrival, he tried calling both Alaska and Sophia one more time, but he didn't still didn't have any lucking reaching them.

"What's up," Ricky asked as soon as he walked through the door of Santee's study.

"I need you to send somebody by Sophia's house to check on her. She left here angry at me last night and now I can't seem to reach her."

"Sure," Ricky replied. "Do you need anything else, sir?"

"Send someone by Alaska's house too," Santee' added. "And have whoever you send call me the moment they get there so I can figure out what the hell is going on."

"Yes sir."

As Ricky quickly exited the room on his way to go and fulfill his request, Santee' cut the end of one of his favorite cigars before lighting it and taking a pull. The smoke calmed him as it entered into his lungs. He briefly closed his eyes, enjoying the moment. Santee' stood up and walked over to the bay window. As he peered down to the garden below, he wondered if he'd done the right thing by proposing to Alaska. Although he truly loved her, he knew better than to think that he could build a foundation from a pile of lies. But when Sophia finally confessed to him the true details surrounding Omar's murder, Santee's was already knee deep in his feelings for Alaska.

He already felt bad for her circumstances, but he felt even worst when he found out that his very own children had been the ones to blame. The guilt he felt over that, along with the fact that he truly did love her, made Santee's desire to be the one to take care of her even stronger. Santee' looked down at his watch. Sophia lived about thirty minutes from his house so he was expecting his phone to ring any minute with an update. As if his men were reading his mind, the phone began to ring and Santee' rushed back over to his desk to answer it.

"Talk to me," he said his heart beating fast as he spoke into the receiver.

"Umm ... hel ... hello sir," the voice of one of his soldiers came over the line. His tone was dripping with fear and Santee' could tell he was terrified to say whatever it was he needed to say.

"Spit it out," he demanded as he yelled at the man on the other end of the line.

"Sir... I'm sorry, but Sophia is dead."

The words took the air out of Santee' chest and he fell back into his chair.

"Find out who did this to my baby girl and bring them to me."

Without another word, Santee' hung up the phone. He was angry as he sat there trying to figure out who would have the balls to murder his daughter. Remembering that Sophia brought a date with her last night to the party, Santee' decided to look over the security tapes to see if he saw anything fishy. Realizing there was just too much footage for him to sort through; Santee' narrowed the playback search to the last hour of the party. That way he would be able to review the minutes leading up too, and directly following Sophia's angry exit. Santee narrowed his search even further by selecting only views from the cameras located in the backyard, driveway, and outside of his study.

After about ten minutes of combing through the video feed, Santee' came to the clip that showed Sophia walking into his study. Realizing that that was where he'd seen her last, Santee' slowed the video playback down to normal speed. Unable to see what he already knew was going on inside the room, Santee' watched the screen as it displayed an empty hallway. He was waiting to see Sophia emerge from the room so that he could follow her movement and hopefully pick up some clues. As he clicked the button to speed up the playback a little faster, Santee' quickly clicked it again when a figured popped up on the screen. Pausing the feed, Santee' zoomed in on the figure's face.

"Alaska?"

Santee' leaned back in his chair as everything began to make sense. He realized that if Alaska overheard their conversation last night, she now knew everything. He also knew it wasn't a coincidence that Sophia was dead.

He wanted to be angry that Alaska had killed his daughter, but knew he couldn't. Although he loved her, Sophia rolled the dice by playing a dirty game of love and murder, and a part of him felt like she deserved whatever fate she got.

Now that everything was out in the open, Santee' needed to see Alaska now more than ever. He wanted to apologize for the secrets he'd held and for the actions of his children. Deciding to go out and look for her himself, Santee' grabbed the keys to his car and headed for the door. Just then, the phone on his desk began to ring and he rushed back to answer it.

"Hey Khalil, what's up?" Santee' said checking the caller ID before picking up the phone. He wasn't sure what his accountant was calling him for on Sunday morning but whatever it was, he needed him to hurry up.

"Hey, sorry to call you during non-business hours but I just needed to get your approval on something."

"Sure. What is it?"

"I spoke with Alaska this morning and she requested a transfer of five million dollars to an off shore account. Since she told me you were in an important meeting, I went ahead and did it for her, but I still wanted to make you aware."

Santee's blood began to boil as he listened to Khalil's words. He had been ready to forgive Alaska for exacting her rightful revenge on his daughter, but Santee' drew the line at her stealing his money.

"Are you fucking crazy?" Santee's spazzed out as he looked at the phone, "Why the fuck would you move that much of my money without my permission."

"I'm sorry," Khalil stuttered. "I thought since she was your fiancée now that it would be okay."

"Reverse the transaction," Santee' said shaking his head. He liked Khalil, but the young boy had just signed his own death certificate with the dumb move he'd just made.

"I can't do that. The transaction has already cleared."

"Well do what the fuck I pay you to do and use her deposit information to transfer it back."

"Uh... just a minute. Let me see if that will work."

Santee' waited as he listened to Khalil type something into the computer.

"The account show's a zero balance. She must have moved the money somewhere else as soon as it cleared."

Santee' slammed the phone down in frustration. The woman he loved had just killed his daughter and walked away into the fucking sunset with $5 million dollars of his money.

"What part of the fucking game is this," Santee' said as he rushed out the door in search of Alaska.

Alaska, Jay and Mo B, all boarded the Boeing 757 airliner as it prepared to take off in route to Trinidad and Tobago. The sun was shining bright as Alaska stared out the window into the bright blue sky. Her thoughts turned to Omar as she thought about everything she's been through in the last few months and she wished that he was still here. Even though she found out he'd cheated on her, Alaska still loved him just as much as she did before, and she blew a kiss up to the sky to remind him. Turning her attention back to the boys, Alaska smiled as she watched Mo B put their bags in the overhead bins. Noticing the faraway look in her eyes, Jay came over and sat next to her.

"How are you holding up?" he asked, placing his hand lovingly on her knee.

"I'm good. I'm just ready for this plane to take off so I can put all this bullshit behind me."

"Well it shouldn't be too much longer sis," Jay smiled as he sat back and fastened his seat belt.

When Alaska woke up this morning, she had thirty-four missed calls from Jay, and she decided to call him back to tell him she was leaving. After she told him everything that happened, Jay dropped a bombshell of his own telling her about Andraya's betrayal. Alaska was shocked, but she wasn't surprised. With everything she'd gone through in the last few months, she'd learned that betrayal was the new norm now, and loyalty was scarce. The only redeeming thing that showed in Draya's actions was the fact that she sent Alaska the information she'd learned about Big Hank before she died.

Alaska didn't have time to get at Hank herself since she knew it wouldn't be long before Santee' came looking for her. So she paid an old friend to do it for her instead. Since Hank had a thing for women and cocaine, Alaska sent her big booty friend Jackie his way with a batch of bad cocaine and a vendetta, knowing he would be dead by the time the sun came up.

The seat belt sign over their heads lit up and Alaska smiled as she clicked hers together. The pilot's voice came over the speaker announcing their departure and the plane slowly began to move. As it rolled down the runway, Alaska found herself staring out the window. She watched aimlessly as the concrete beneath them rolled by. The plane stopped rolling, lining itself up perfectly with the runway, and that's when Alaska saw him.

Standing next to his car which was parked on the runway, Santee' watched as the plane took off.

Once they were in the air, Alaska breathed a sigh of relief. But that relief was short lived as she looked down at the text that had just come to her phone. It was from Santee' and it read;

See you in Trinidad and Tobago, BITCH!

To be continued....

ORDER FORM

$14.99 $14.99 $14.99   COMING SOON

COMING SOON   COMING SOON   COMING SOON   COMING SOON

  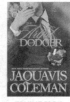 

COMING SOON   COMING SOON   COMING SOON   COMING SOON

COMING SOON

Wholesale orders: $6.75 + shipping (Minimum of 20 books)
Inmate Orders: $12.00 + Free shipping
Book Club Orders (minimum order of 10 books): $12.75 + shipping

WHOLESALE ORDERS CAN BE PLACED AT OWLBOOKORDERS@HOTMAIL.COM

TITLE   QTY   NAME _____
                           (Include Prison #)

_____ _____   SHIP TO_____

_____ _____

_____ _____   MAIL FORM TO:
                           OWL Book Orders
_____ _____   PO Box 181048
     TOTAL _____   Utica, MI 48318